DARK
PROMISE

DARK PROMISE

DARKHAVEN SAGA: BOOK THREE

DANIELLE ROSE

WATERHOUSE PRESS

ISBN: 978-1-64263-169-2

For Shawna—
for always having my back and extending that whip.
You make me a better writer.
This one is for you.

ONE

There's a moment in one's life when everything changes irrevocably. It's usually after an awful decision. I don't think we're usually privy to the timing of this moment. It happens, we react, and we must deal with the consequences.

Somehow, I know this is that moment for me, yet I can't stop myself from running steadfast into the unknown. After everything—the promises that were broken and the lies that were told, after I was forsaken and abused by the very people who shared my life's blood—I am still tethered to them.

I can't see our link. If I could, I would break it. I would cut it into a million pieces so no one could braid it again. I can't see it, but I know it's there, tying my soul to theirs. I want to break free, to run wild with my vampire clan, but I can't. I'm secured to the ground, rooted in place, until someone speaks.

"Liv is missing, *mija,*" *Mamá* says, her voice soft, her eyes tired.

I stare at them in silence. The moonlight casts shadows across their faces, distorting their features into hellish expressions. In this light, they look like monsters.

They don't want to be here, but they've come seeking my aid. For months, I wanted nothing more than to end our feud. I truly believed we could have peace. After all, we fight for the same cause—to stop rogue vampires—but then I dreamed about a spell gone awry. Mamá cut me, sinking her dagger into my flesh. My arm still aches where blade met bone.

Of course, this never happened, but I feel it as sharply as I feel the cold wind against my face and the crunch of frozen ground beneath my feet. I hold my arm against my chest, rubbing a wound that never existed in reality. I tell myself that was only a dream. But was it?

I may be undead now, but I was born a spirit witch with an affinity for clairvoyance. This isn't the first time a dream morphed into something more, something solid I can fight. After I woke from the nightmare, I was of the firm belief that the witches were up to no good. Now I must decide if my premonition is coming true. Are they here for retribution and vengeance?

But Liv is missing.

A rogue vampire has taken her, and it's only a matter of time before she becomes a meal or something worse… Something like me.

A witch-turned-vampire is a curious creature. I am not vampire, not witch, but both. I have one foot firmly planted in both worlds, yet I belong to neither.

As I think about what my former best friend must be experiencing, I feel ill. I was blessed to have been saved by Jasik and his comrades. Unlike rogues, my saviors follow a set of unspoken guidelines to maintain peace and anonymity— like not eating people. It's generally considered poor form to do so.

I know Liv isn't as lucky, and if she has been taken, she's running out of time.

My mind is a mess, my emotions clouding my judgment. I replay Mamá's words over and over again. Each time, I still don't know if I can believe her. Is this another lie? After the witches' last betrayal, I vowed never to return to my old life, never to aid them or fight on their side again. I fell asleep yesterday believing I was free, but I woke to another nightmare.

"Will you help us?" someone asks.

Among the witches is Liv's mother. Her eyes are bloodshot and sunken, her skin pale and wrinkled. Her nose is pink, her lips dry. Her dull hair is frizzy and flutters in the breeze. She shivers from the cold and wraps her arms around her chest.

Liv's mother never liked me or my coven, but the two seem to have merged into a single covenant. Their intention is to protect Darkhaven, the small village we all call home, from those who keep to the shadows. I once fought beside them, but now I see their prejudice has blinded them from the truth.

Not all vampires are evil, soulless fiends who need to be sent straight to hell.

I find it ironic that Liv and her family are intent on killing us. In the past, Liv had to sneak out just to see me. Her mother, a self-professed flower child and free spirit, didn't believe in violence. Now she joins the fight as often as she can—and so does Liv.

I saved her from a rogue vampire just last night, and he's dead. So how is she missing? Who took her? What happened after I left the witches?

"Perhaps she ran away?" I say, finally speaking. While unlike Liv, this is the most obvious conclusion. The rogues from that nest are supposed to be dead.

"*No seas tonta, niña,*" Mamá chastises.

"I'm not being foolish, Mamá," I say. "This doesn't make sense. The rogues are *gone*, so who could have taken her?"

"There are always more vampires! Don't be naïve," Liv's mother says.

In the distance, something catches my eye. The woods are eerily dark tonight, and even the moonlight struggles to find its way through the thick branches. I squint at a shadow. It moves when I focus on it, returning behind the base of a thick tree.

"Someone is out there," I say.

I rush forward, pushing past the witches. Mamá grabs on to my arm, yanking me backward. She squeezes me tightly in the very spot her dagger slid into my flesh. The raw sensation of her angry glare and bony fingers sends shivers down my spine. Being a naturally stronger predator, I pull free easily and step backward, putting space between the witches and me. I hold on to my arm, rubbing my skin. I don't like the feel of her skin against mine. Not only because of the hell she put me through since I've transitioned but also because mortals are scorching to the touch. I still feel the heat of her body on mine. It takes several seconds for the sensation to dissipate.

"*No te preocupes por eso,*" she says, but I do worry. Someone is watching us, and whoever it is might know what happened to Liv. I live in a particularly deserted part of the forest. The only people this far into the woods either reside here with me or are looking for trouble. And this isn't the former.

I glance back at the woods, and I see a set of eyes staring back at me. The unsettling feeling that I'm being watched washes over me, and all at once, I realize how vulnerable I am. I'm standing in the forest with known enemies. I'm alone, my only allies inside Amicia's nest, the Victorian-style manor behind me, waiting for my call.

I recognize the onlooker as a member of Mamá's coven. It's distressing to know there are more witches hiding behind trees, but I don't show my fear. The witches need to understand that bringing the fight to our doorstep will never end well for them. We are at our most powerful here, and an attack would be fatal to them.

Maneuvering through the overgrown yard, I backpedal until my heels knock into the steps of our wraparound porch. I take each one at a time, never breaking eye contact with our unexpected visitors. I'm so distracted, I almost forget to pat our watcher—an old stone gargoyle perched on the top step—on his head. This has become a ritual for me. I reach for him, running my hand along his smooth scalp.

As I bend over, the necklace I was hiding under my shirt falls loose and dangles atop my black T-shirt. The chain glistens in the moonlight. Prominently featured, the silver cross is shimmery against my shirt. Its sparkle catches the eyes of the witches, who gasp.

"*Eso no es posible,*" Mamá says. The other witches mimic her response, shouting that it's not possible for a vampire to touch such a sacred object. Internally, I agree with them. Vampires cannot touch crosses. Jasik just proved that to me.

But I'm not *just* a vampire.

I'm something more, something *better*.

"What are you?" someone hisses, her voice betraying her disgust with all that I am.

They may not know everything, but they have witnessed some of my peculiar traits. In addition to my newfound ability to touch religious relics, I also have access to magic—and not just *any* magic. The power within me is pure, formidable. It's like nothing I've ever felt before.

I've wielded this magic in several attacks against rogue vampires, and the witches watched as my enemies were turned to ash by my mere touch. My hands contain the very flames of the fiery depths of hell, and I will eagerly use this magic to aid my comrades.

The witches act surprised now, but I wonder how shocked they really are. They know I can use magic. They've seen it with their own eyes. Wouldn't they expect more from me? Did they come here to ask for my help because they want to see what else I can do? Is this why they're here now, begging for help? Just yesterday, they wanted nothing to do with me. Now they consider me an ally. They trust me to save one of their own?

I grab my cross pendant, trailing my fingers over the cool metal. Rather than harm me, it gives me strength. I was given this necklace by *Papá* before he died, and since Mamá has stolen my stake, this cross is all I have left of him.

"How is this possible?" someone asks.

"Because the world is not just black and white," I say. "Nothing is ever that simple. You condemn us all based on the actions of a few. That's not fair or right. Even this cross trusts in me, so why can't you?"

I tuck my necklace back under my shirt, letting the metal slide against my bare skin. It tickles as it slides down to its rightful place between my clavicles, but it does not burn me. The only thing that stings is the way Mamá looks at me, her only child, with such disdain. She hates what I am, but I see the wheels turning behind her narrowed gaze. She's up to something.

"Are you certain you want the vampires' help?" I ask. I need to hear them say it aloud, especially *her*. The witches have come to the vampires for help. *They* need *us*. I won't agree until they realize it.

Mamá's eyes are hard. They're so dark brown, they're almost black. Our eyes used to be identical, right down to their shape. Now my irises are crimson—the same color as the blood of the innocent. Or, in my case, the blood from blood bags.

"We can find her without you," Mamá says.

"But you can't *stop* them," I clarify. "Not without us."

The witches know I'm right. This isn't about who's naturally stronger or who's the better fighter—both titles go to the vampires, though. This is about putting aside our differences to save someone. To stop the rogues. This is about protecting Darkhaven.

"And you speak for everyone?" Mamá asks.

I shake my head. "No. I make no decisions for anyone. We agree together, as a *family*."

Mamá narrows her eyes. It was petty of me to say the vampires are my family now, but I couldn't stop myself. In the past few months, these vampires have been more of a family to me than Mamá ever was. They trusted me, trained me, and even risked their lives for me. They believed in me when no one else did.

Mamá never respected me or my power. She never believed in me. Sure, she loved me. I was her daughter after all. She's not totally heartless, but in her eyes, I was a novice compared to her. Now the student has become the master, and she must admit it.

"*No tenemos tiempo para esto*," Mamá says.

"You will *make* time, Mamá."

I know I've upset her. Her hands are balled into fists at her sides. Her jaw is clenched, her eyes narrowed. Her nostrils flare with every sharp inhalation. She wants to tear me down. She wants me to submit to her. Before I was a vampire, I wouldn't dare betray her. Not like this. Especially not in front of her peers. Everything I did, I did for the coven.

But I'm not that girl anymore.

"Do you want our help?" I ask again, emphasizing each word.

There is a long pause, and then she says, "Yes. I want your help."

She is seething, her anger almost to its boiling point. Before she can erupt and ruin our unexpected truce, I smile.

"I need a minute," I say.

I turn and face the manor. Two large double doors welcome me home, and I can see several blurred figures standing behind the stained glass.

The vampires are waiting inside. No doubt they've been listening to our chat, and they know I'm coming in to convince them we should help. I know they'll be upset with me. Just yesterday, I promised this was over. I assured them I had no intention of helping the witches ever again.

I meant the promise I made, but this is different. It's not about Mamá or the coven. This time, Liv is missing—Liv, the weak firestarter who begged for my help because her mother wouldn't let her practice magic in the house.

I've known Liv all my life. In fact, I can't remember a time I *didn't* know her. That bond is special. She may hate what I am, but she can't label me a monster. I've yet to do something deserving of that title.

So I twist the knob and walk into the foyer. Closing the door behind me, I shut out the witches and stare into the crimson irises of several angry nestmates.

Surrounded by vampires, the space feels small, suffocating. I step backward until I'm flush against the stained-glass door. At my right, a doorway opens to the parlor, which is just a fancy word for our living room. Straight ahead is the sitting room, which connects to the dining room, solarium, and upstairs. Everywhere I look, I see vampires staring at me. No one looks happy.

"Do I really need to point out that this is a horrible idea?" Hikari asks. She's leaning against the doorframe that connects the foyer to the parlor. She glares at me, her arms crossed over her chest. Her black pixie locks are messy, the gelled spikes granting a defiant edge to her looks.

"If anyone else was missing, I wouldn't ask this of you," I say.

"You made a promise, Ava," Jeremiah says. He stands beside Hikari, his right leg kicked back so the sole of his shoe rests against the wall. He fingers the zipper of his jacket as he stares at me. His dark skin is ashy, and his eyes are hard. He looks exhausted. I'm certain that has something to do with Holland, his ex-boyfriend who is now living with us.

"I know, and I hate to break that promise," I say.

I don't dare look at Malik. Since I transitioned, he's become too brotherly, and I know my request to aid the witches will only disappoint him. The last thing I want to do is upset him, seeing as how he's also my trainer. Last time, he took out his frustrations with my bad decisions while we were on the mat. I felt sore for the rest of that week.

Jasik and Malik have one striking characteristic in common: they're practically unreadable emotionally. I take a peek at the vampire standing beside me. His eyes are hard, cold. I know Jasik is upset with me. It seems like I'm choosing the witches over the vampires—*again*—but I'm not.

"Liv was my best friend," I explain. "She's seventeen and far too weak to handle herself against rogues. She won't survive."

"And why do we care?" Hikari asks.

"Hikari," Jasik scolds, his tone sharp.

"No, let her say what we're all thinking," Jeremiah says.

"But I feel responsible." My voice is whiny as I admit defeat.

"Why?" Hikari asks. "You did everything you could to stop the rogues. You owe them nothing."

"She's right, Ava," Amicia says. Finally, our fearless leader speaks. Her silence was unnerving, and her impassive gaze made it difficult to tell if she was going to side with me or her vampires. I should have known she'd pick them.

"No, I mean, she never wanted to be a fighter. She never wanted to hunt vampires. She only did that to help *me*. She went on patrols with me so I wouldn't be alone, so I'd always have someone to count on."

Amicia is only a few feet away from me. With arms crossed, her index finger taps to the tick of a nearby grandfather clock. The *tap, tap, tap* of her disapproving finger echoes in my mind. I try to assess her thoughts by reading her eyes, but she's just as detached as the others. One thing older vampires are exceptionally good at is perfecting that expressionless gaze.

Finally, she speaks. "And because of this, you feel responsible for her abduction? You have no control over the rogues. They do as they please."

"This isn't about the rogues. Don't you see that? The only reason Liv was there last night is because of me. I brought her into this. I took her hunting the night this all started. They wouldn't even know about her or her connection to me if it wasn't for what I did."

My tone is testy, my emotions irritable—a volatile combination for an already cranky vampire.

"That's a bit of a stretch, Ava," Jeremiah says.

"You can't blame yourself for this," Malik adds.

They speak almost in unison.

I groan internally. How can I better explain this to them? If I don't sway them to my side, they won't agree to find Liv, and I know the witches can't do this alone. They might be able to *find* her, but they'll never fight off an entire nest.

"They don't deserve our help," Hikari says. Her tone is absolute.

I know there's no convincing her, but I try anyway. "Liv doesn't deserve to die just because her coven is ungrateful."

"I don't trust them, Ava," Amicia says. Her tone is sharp, calm.

"I don't either," I admit. "But Liv needs our help."

"How can you be sure this isn't a setup?" Amicia asks. Sometimes I think she's a mind reader. I know this is impossible, but she so accurately conveys my own thoughts far too often for my liking.

I shrug. "I can't, but regardless, I won't risk Liv's life on the off chance they're lying."

"That is what they do best," Hikari says under her breath.

Amicia shoots her a look that makes my stomach queasy. Hikari silences immediately and stands straighter, no longer slouching against the doorframe. This makes me smile. There's something about Amicia that makes my insides flutter in all the worst ways. She radiates power like the sun does heat. Jasik explained that it's her age. The older the vampire, the more powerful the vampire, and Amicia is as old as they come. It's comforting to know I'm not the only one who submits to her will so easily.

"You have far too many admirable qualities, Ava," Amicia

says. "These witches never deserved you."

I smile, relief washing over me. I thought it was going to be much harder to convince them to help.

"But I will not risk our lives again. My answer is no."

Amicia's words roar through the silent house. No one speaks—not me, not the other vampires, not the witches outside. For one brief moment in time, her words are comforting. She grants me the one thing I could never get on my own: freedom from the witches.

Then I blink back into reality.

TWO

The solarium is dark.

The clouds roll in, and the stars hide behind this overcast evening. The moonlight doesn't quite penetrate the endless row of stained-glass windows like it does on other nights. It's as if the sky knows what's happening—the eerie request from the witches startling it, too.

Amicia and I are alone. She ordered the vampires to retreat to their bedchambers and the hunters to wait in the foyer, leaving just the two of us alone to chat. I don't have a good feeling about this.

I glance through the parlor and spot my sire by the front door. Jasik eyes me curiously, anxiously awaiting our return. The others don't make eye contact. They're not happy with me or this situation. They want the witches to leave and for life to get back to normal, but our enemies have no intention of leaving us—not until I join them outside and share the bad news.

Even then, I may have to *force* them to leave. The witches came seeking aid. I doubt they'll just walk away without help, especially with such a precious life hanging in the balance.

Amicia made it clear. We will not aid them. We will not look for Liv. By choosing to remain part of this vampire family, I have condemned my past to death. That stark realization doesn't startle me.

When I asked Jasik to save me—when I willingly became a vampire—I knew I would be forced to choose. Deep down, that reality lived inside me. I fought it over the months that passed, striving for a world without violence and bloodshed. Now I know the truth. Utopia only exists in my dreams. Unfortunately, when I close my eyes, I don't envision that perfect world; I see nightmares of betrayal and hatred instead.

The tiny hairs all over my body alert me to something sinister. My throat tightens, and in the corner of my eye, I see her. Amicia is standing close beside me. She follows my gaze, and Jasik quickly looks away. He's pretending not to be eavesdropping. They all are. Amicia narrows her gaze before speaking.

"Wait outside with our visitors," she says. Her tone is sharp, abrupt, leaving no room for argument.

Jasik nods and offers me a quick farewell glance. One by one, the hunters step onto the porch. The door is closed firmly behind them, and I've never felt more alone. I know I'm safe here. Amicia has admitted that she cares for me and wants me to remain a member of her nest, but still, something about this situation is unsettling.

Why can't the hunters eavesdrop? Asking them to wait outside, knowing they will be too distracted to focus on our conversation while the witches are so close, seems as though our fearless leader has malicious intentions. I try not to think about that. I don't want to visualize more treachery. A girl can only handle so much deception and dishonesty before she begins to take it personally.

"I know you're upset with me," I say. I'm the first to speak, and I do so softly. I'm cautious because I don't want to upset her. Not simply for personal safety, but also because I do cherish my life here.

I scan the room, looking for the best seating. Being the only two vampires in the room, we have our choice, but I want to be in earshot of the hunters outside. I don't trust that the witches won't see this as a preemptive strike against them. They're paranoid enough to make matters worse.

There are several wooden benches lining the walls, and Amicia takes a seat at one. She ushers for me to join her. I hesitate before sitting directly beside her. Our legs touch, and the sensation of brushing against something so cold and solid jolts my heart.

Amicia has an unexpected strength to her aura—one that permeates into the space surrounding her. *Everyone* can feel it, even the witches. With her being so small and frail-looking, it's jarring to feel threatened or scared of her, but she's the strongest vampire I've ever met. Time allots the undead many things—the enhanced strength is probably the most coveted.

We're similar in height, and once I unlock my full power, we just might be similar in vitality and vigor. But I'd never dare challenge Amicia—not unless I must, that is.

I don't look at her. Instead, I eye the many open seats. With all the vampires elsewhere, this house has never felt so empty, so lonely. In addition to the benches, there are several tables and ottomans. Plants that thrive in the darkness clutter the space, making it difficult to assess how massive this room truly is, but it lines the entire right side of the manor.

The solarium is my favorite room in the house, which I find intriguing. In theory, this room is for sun worshippers, not vampires. And even before I transitioned, I was always a night owl. I've never cared for sunshine or early mornings or sunrises.

But I could watch a sunset until my retinas burned. Only when the sun finally slumbers and the world is blanketed in darkness do I truly feel alive. There's something special about the night. It speaks to me in ways the light never did, never could. Sometimes I believe I was born to be a vampire, for I find my strength in the shadows. I've always been an outcast, a misfit, and I've never felt more loved, or more comfortable in my own skin, until I became one of them.

"I'm not upset with you, Ava," Amicia says. Her voice is soft, clear, and completely unreadable.

I groan internally. I don't believe her, but why would she lie? I'm beginning to think the witches' paranoia is seeping into the house.

"I don't want to help the witches," I confess. This isn't a total lie.

"Are you sure?" she asks.

"I just... I don't want Liv to die." My voice is whisper soft and utterly vulnerable. I don't miss the difference between Amicia, a leader, and me, a follower. Mamá used to think I would one day lead our coven. I laugh at the thought now.

If I've learned nothing else from my time with the vampires, I've learned I'm too rash to be a leader. I would charge into battle headstrong and watch my followers die. Look at what's happening right now. If it were up to me, I would help the witches. Amicia must sense something I do not.

"I know she was your friend," Amicia says.

I nod. "We were best friends."

"But you're not anymore," she explains, her voice deadpan.

"I know." This is beginning to feel strangely like an interrogation.

"Do you?"

I arch a brow and decide not to beat around the bush. "What do you mean?"

"Do you understand that you're no longer friends with these people?"

I shrug and play with loose threads dangling from the edge of my top. I pull some free and roll them into little balls between the pads of my fingertips.

"You're hindered by your emotions, Ava, but one day, you'll see that I made the right decision."

I exhale sharply and drop the threads onto the tile floor. "I'm tired of everyone assuming I'm an emotional mess. I'm not a child. I make decisions based on what's right, and leaving Liv to die is just plain wrong."

"You are blinded by your loyalty to them," Amicia says. "This is why you cannot see the wisdom of my choice not to aid them."

I shake my head. "You're wrong. You just don't want to help them because of everything that's happened."

"They are our enemy."

"We've all made mistakes, but we must break this cycle," I say. "We can have a better life here."

"You make empty promises of eternal peace. This will never happen, Ava. Don't you see that? The witches will never be our allies."

I scoff. "Don't you think you're being a little hypocritical?"

"Excuse me?" Her eyes narrow.

"When you needed assistance to learn more about my magic, you turned to a witch. You asked Holland to come here, to help me control my magic. How is that any different?" I cross my arms over my chest, and the top of my shirt crinkles. My cross necklace is exposed. The silver metal glistens in the light, catching Amicia's eye.

"Holland has proven his devotion to us. Never has he endangered my vampires. You gave your witches every opportunity to work with us, and each time, they disappointed you. Why do you allow them to continue hurting you?"

I exhale loudly and drop my hands into my lap. "They're scared. That's all. I don't know if you've noticed, but mortals tend to lash out at what they don't understand."

Amicia snorts. "Oh, I've noticed."

I never forget how many years she's been walking this earth, and it never ceases to amaze me. If she didn't give me the complete wiggins, I would ask Amicia about her time here. Where was she born? How did she die? Did she know what was happening to her? Does she miss her family? I'm guessing she doesn't. If she did, she'd give me the opportunity to salvage my relationships with my remaining blood relatives.

"Eventually they'll understand that we're the good guys," I say. "They just need more time to see past their prejudice."

Amicia holds up her hand, silencing me. "Enough. I have an eternity on this planet, Ava, and I still wouldn't offer the witches even one moment of it. They don't deserve my leniency, and they certainly don't deserve your loyalty."

I sigh, defeated. Amicia and I will never agree on this. She's seen far too many horrendous acts to forgive the witches of their misdeeds, and the witches are too stubborn to believe a vampire can truly be good. This is a vicious cycle that won't end even in our lifetime.

"So what happens now?" I ask.

"You will tell the witches that we will not aid them, and you will make it clear that another unannounced visit is unacceptable. I will agree to only one pact: they stay off our property, and we'll stay away from theirs."

"And if they don't listen?"

Amicia doesn't answer, but her eyes say everything my ears don't hear. If the witches come here again, she will be their end. The coven might be powerful, but Amicia is an experienced fighter. I'm certain she will outsmart even the most ruthless coven.

She glances down at my neckline, but my cross is covered by my shirt. In the morning rush, I didn't have time to show her my new ability, but I'm sure someone else mentioned it while I was outside with the witches. I wait for the proper time to pull out a cross—one of the few things that can cause everlasting physical pain to a vampire—and shove it in her face as a declaration of my strength. Fidgeting in my seat, I'm uneasy with the idea.

"Ava, I'm going to ask you to do something that might make you uncomfortable."

I swallow hard. "What is it?" Inside, I'm screaming, begging her not to make me hurt the witches. I've already turned my back on them—and my former best friend. Isn't that enough? Can't we end this here, now?

"Vampires make blood promises to each other. I want you to make this promise to me now," Amicia says. As she speaks, everything about her—from her voice to her eyes to her face—is void of emotion. She blinks, waiting for my response.

"What am I promising?" I ask, confused.

"You must promise not to search for the witch on your own. Promise that you will respect my decision." She sits back, resting against the bench's armrest, and folds her hands in her lap. With her fingers laced together, her back straight, her head high, she's awfully threatening.

"And what do I have to do?" I ask softly. I'm cowering under her gaze, finding it difficult to simply look her in the eyes when she speaks.

"You must make a blood oath to me, to this family. You are one of us, Ava, regardless of who sired you."

"A blood oath?" I ask. My voice quivers, betraying my hesitation.

"I understand this is unfamiliar to you, but this is something vampires do." She gives me a Cheshire cat smile. It's wide, large, and emotionless.

Completely creeped out, I look down at my hands. "Jasik's never mentioned blood promises before," I say, thinking back to all the times he explained how different the vampire lifestyle will be for me. Surprisingly to both of us, vampires and witches aren't that different. Discovering the witches have been lying to me about a lot of things for a very long time was a difficult cross to bear. Yet, I've forgiven all the atrocities they've committed against me, against us.

But I'm finding it hard to trust Amicia now. I remind myself that she's been more of a mother to me than my own blood. She's kept me safe, offered me refuge, given me food... And I doubt her now?

I nod, trying to convince myself I'm doing the right thing. "Okay. I'll do it."

Amicia smiles again, but this time, her eyes slant in a mischievous stare. I swallow hard as she reaches for my hand. "Wise decision, my child."

The moments that follow rush in an uncomfortable haze. I'm completely aware of everything I'm doing, but I don't feel as though the actions are my own. It's like I'm floating above my body, watching as something else controls my movements.

Whatever this thing is, it's the one who's obeying Amicia's orders, and it's using my body to do it.

"Hold your hand like this," Amicia says. She places her hand before me, palm facing the ceiling. I mimic her action. "This shouldn't hurt."

Her fingernails are painted black, and she digs a pointed tip into my flesh until a deep crimson liquid pools in my hand. I wince as she burrows deeper, the pain stinging through my hand and radiating up my arm. I gnaw on my lower lip until I draw blood. I suck down several droplets before my skin can heal.

When she withdraws, her nail is coated in my blood. No longer black, it drips off her finger and splashes into the puddle that's formed in my palm.

She assaults her own palm in much the same way before grabbing on to me. Our palms pressed tightly together, we interlock fingers, and she speaks.

"Give me your blood oath, Ava," Amicia orders.

"I—I promise... I promise I won't go after the witch by myself," I say, stumbling over my words. What exactly does one say when making a blood oath?

Amicia's mouth presses into a firm line, but she relents. I guess I did it correctly after all.

"Very good," she says.

She pulls her hand free of my grip and licks her palm clean. Nauseated by her actions, I just stare at mine. The wound has healed, but the blood remains. Clenching my hand, I smear it with my fingers, only succeeding in making a mess. I wipe my hand on my jeans, but even with a clean hand, I can still feel her blood there. I still feel the moment her fingernail tore through my flesh, and I feel her blood coursing through my veins. It makes me uneasy and downright dirty. Somehow, I know I've just betrayed my sire.

"I don't understand."

"We can't help you," I repeat.

The witches have surrounded us, but thankfully, the other hunters are behind me. No longer hiding behind the solid front door, they stand at my sides, forming an impenetrable line should the witches attempt to force their way inside. Of course, they wouldn't do that. There's nothing for them here.

Jasik is next to me, and he grabs on to my hand, linking his fingers with mine. I swallow a knot in my throat and relish in his strength. He makes me more courageous and self-assured.

Suddenly, I realize I'm not nervous because of the witches. They'll be upset with my decision, but they will accept it. The witches will leave, and the vampires will return to the manor, to their sire.

My throat is tight and raspy because of the dark promise Amicia forced me to make. Jasik's skin is resting against my palm—the very same one that swore a blood oath to another vampire. My stomach curls in response. If I tense, Jasik pretends not to notice.

"You would condemn your friend?" Liv's mother asks me. She looks at me like she's finally seeing the monster she believes I've become.

Standing straighter and with a firm voice, I say, "Liv is not my friend anymore."

"And I suppose we are no longer your family?" Mamá asks.

I shake my head. "No, not anymore." My voice is faint, but I know she hears me. Jasik caresses my skin with his thumb, and I soften a little, taking a deep breath and clearing my thoughts. First, I deal with the witches. Later, I'll figure out what that blood oath entails.

"How can you say that?" Liv's mother shouts. She doesn't hide her disgust. Like her temper, her frizzy hair whips out at me with even a subtle breeze.

Mamá gasps, shaking her head. "*Qué te han hecho?*"

Instantly angry by Mamá's words, I lash out, withholding nothing. "What have they done to me? Do you want the truth, Mamá? They've loved me, supported me, protected me… They've done everything you were supposed to do as my mother!"

"*Cállate, niña!*" Mamá shouts. "Do you think these beasts truly care for you?"

"I know they do." I squeeze Jasik's hand, and he returns the sensation. Lifting our interlocked hands, I rest our fists against my chest.

"*Eres un tonto,*" Mamá says.

"I'm no fool, Mamá. For once, I see the truth," I say. I lower my arms so our hands are back at our sides.

"*De qué estás hablando?*"

"I'm talking about how you never cared about me, Mamá." Tears are hot and sticky behind my lids. They pool in my eyes, but I don't care. I need the witches to see that they did this to themselves. They made their bed, and now they must lie in it. If only they had accepted me and been kind to the vampires, they wouldn't be alone now. Their prejudice is costing Liv her life, but that is their sacrifice, not mine.

Never fond of dramatic behavior, Mamá rolls her eyes,

waving off my heavy emotions.

"I tried to help you. How many times did I come to your house? How many times did I save you from the rogues? You told me never to return," I say, throat coarse.

"*No dije eso,*" Mamá says.

Sniffling, I wipe away the single tear that escapes my hold. "You're right. You didn't say that. *Liv said that.* But you didn't stop her, and you let me leave."

"You don't belong there anymore," Mamá says.

I nod. "I know. I belong here."

Mamá shakes her head. "Don't do this, *mija.* Come with us. Help us find her."

I frown. Why is she trying so hard to convince me to go with them? An itchy sensation is making its way from my heart to my brain. This is starting to feel like a setup.

"No," I say firmly.

"Let's go, Tatiana," Liv's mother says as she glances at my mother.

Mamá looks at me with disappointment in her eyes. "We thought you would help because—"

"Because she was your *best friend*," Liv's mother interrupts.

"She was, but you said it yourself. My place is here. I don't belong with you anymore."

With one final glance, Mamá turns on her heels and leaves. The witches follow, each offering single glances of disapproval. When they're finally gone, I sigh, releasing tension I didn't realize I was holding.

"Are you okay?" Jasik asks.

"I am," I lie. Not because I want to or because I think he can't handle the truth. I lie because the desire within me to obey Amicia's order is a crushing wave that's suffocating me. I'm drowning in a whirlpool of her words and my promise to abide by them.

THREE

The more distance I put between the manor and me, the better I feel. My head clears, my erratic emotions wane, and I can finally breathe. The ever-constant clutter of Amicia's words no longer swirl in my mind, allowing me to think freely for the first time since this whole mess started.

I was happy—finally, truly happy. I released myself from familial obligations and vowed devotion to the vampires. I was one step closer to a life free of insults and betrayal. And then the witches showed up. Can they sense my happiness? Is that how they always know the best time to ruin my day?

I imagine Mamá has some kind of crystal ball that she stares into, witnessing my private and most cherished moments. Like a tiger hunting a gazelle, she pounces, digging her claws in so deeply, she shatters bone.

I rub my arm, feeling the sharp, cold blade sliding through flesh—*my* flesh. I fear I may never shake that dream, or nightmare, or premonition. Whatever it was, it haunts me. I shake, and Jasik notices. Out of the corner of my eye, I see him watching me. I don't dare look up to him. I don't want him to know just how affected I am by both the witches' request and by my nightmare.

"Is everything okay?" Jasik asks, ignoring my silent plea not to ask me any questions.

I don't respond. I'm not sure what to say. Can I be honest with him? Should I tell him about the blood oath I made to Amicia? Will he be angry that I made a blood promise to someone other than my sire? I don't know anything about this sacrifice, and my naïvety makes me feel uneasy. I was blindsided, given no other option but to submit to her request. Jasik will understand that... right?

He eyes me curiously, his gaze lingering. My breath catches, and my cheeks are warm. The worst part about being this pale is that my formerly tan skin no longer hides my emotions. Mamá used to say I wear my heart on my sleeve, and that definitely hasn't changed, even after death. The only difference is now my own body betrays my secrets.

I turn away from his gaze and pretend to stare into the distance. I act like I'm patrolling, which is the whole point of walking the woods tonight, but hunting is the last thing on my mind. I don't like that we're acting as though nothing happened.

I turned away the witches, and the vampires decided to continue with their scheduled patrols. We're all pretending like we're the only ones in the woods tonight, but I know that's not true. Somewhere out there, the witches are walking home, disappointed in my decision and angry enough to retaliate. Doesn't that bother anyone besides me?

I exhale sharply, stress eating away at my core. I can't stop thinking about Liv. I wonder if she's okay. It's stupid to think about these things, but I need to know if she's hurt, hungry, scared... Silently, I call out to her with my mind. I apologize for abandoning her when she needs me, and I beg her to understand. I have no choice but to follow orders. No longer part of my former coven, I'm not a witch anymore. Of course, my silent prayers fall upon deaf ears. Liv isn't a spirit witch, so she can't respond if she can't hear me.

"I know you're upset," Jasik says. He distracts me from my mental berating long enough for me to welcome my anger once again.

"I am," I admit.

I cross my arms over my chest and kick at the brush beneath my feet. The world is cold, and the ground is hard, crunchy, and layered in frost. The forest is lifeless, but it sparkles. The moonlight glistens across the dead grass and bare trees. Snow can make nature's worst season so beautiful.

"I wish you wouldn't take this decision personally," Jasik says.

I scoff. "How can I not?"

"This has nothing to do with *you*. Amicia made her decision because experience has proven they cannot be trusted."

"Oh, I know… They are *witches*, and we are *vampires*, and there can't possibly be *peace* or *happiness*. There's no such thing as morals because we're *mortal enemies*, right?"

My voice is erratic, my body dramatic. I emphasize my words with the help of frantic hand gestures. I know I'm acting like a child, but this whole situation is ridiculous. I am surrounded by stubborn people who are content living a hellish life fueled by feuds and vengeance. Why can't they see it doesn't have to be this way?

"Ava," Jasik says. He's disappointed in me, and that hurts more than the look on Mamá's face when I told her I wouldn't help find Liv, but I'm too far gone. I'm too wrapped up in my own anger to see through Jasik's words.

"What?" I snap.

"You're not being fair," he says.

Shocked, I stop abruptly and turn to face him. "Seriously?

I'm the one being unfair? You know what's not fair? Letting Liv *die* because of some ridiculous feud!"

"Yes, that's not right either. I regret that the cost of what's happened is your friend's life, but can't you see that you're being a bit childish too?"

I furrow my brows, narrowing my eyes so he understands just how upset I truly am. "Don't you call me childish." I'm pointing my index finger at his chest, and with each word, I jab it into his flesh.

Amusement sparks behind his long lashes, and that makes me even angrier. How can he find this funny? I happen to think this is the worst situation I've ever been in, and I *died* recently. So that's saying *a lot.*

"This isn't funny, Jasik," I say, seething.

"Well—"

"Well *what?*"

"It is *a little* funny." He shows me just how funny he thinks it is with his thumb and index finger.

Exasperated, I exhale sharply and turn on my heel to continue patrolling. "I don't expect you to understand. Do you even *have* a best friend? I mean, when was the last time someone actually wanted to spend time with you as opposed to being forced to courtesy of *Queen* Amicia?"

He stops walking. I don't see him, but I hear the sudden halt of his feet. The untouched snow before him should be marked with his shoe prints, but it's not. The vacant white abyss beside me nearly chokes the life from my body. I turn to face him, immediately regretting my words.

"Jasik..." I shake my head, searching for something to say that would justify my behavior. I went too far. I was too harsh. I can't believe I took out my frustration on the one person I actually care to be around right now.

"It's okay. You're upset," he says, shrugging off my concern as he walks toward me.

He plays it cool, like my words don't affect him, but I see the shock and sadness in his eyes. Pointing out that he has essentially been alone—without his blood family and childhood friends—for far too many years was a low blow on my part. I had no right to be such a jerk. A hundred years from now, the last thing I'd want is to be reminded that everyone I ever loved is dead—and that I'll *never* see them again.

"No, it's not. It's never okay for me to talk to you like that. I didn't mean what I said."

"Vampires live a different life than mortals," Jasik says.

"I know."

"We don't necessarily get to choose our sires or our subsequent obligations after the transition."

What kills me more than that quick flash of pain behind his eyes is the fact that he feels the need to justify himself to me. He doesn't need to explain why he lives the way he lives or why his life has been focused on eradicating rogues rather than making friends.

"I know," I say again. "I'm sorry. I didn't mean it."

"Hunters spend their lives protecting vampires," he continues. "We don't have time to make friends."

I close the space between us and grab his hands. I squeeze them slightly and rub my thumbs over his cool skin. "I'm sorry."

He smiles. "It's okay."

"I'm just upset. I shouldn't have taken it out on you."

He shakes his head. "No, you shouldn't have, but you *should* talk about it."

I pull away from him and step back. "There isn't anything

to talk about."

"Ava, stop this. I'm your *sire*. That's not just some superficial bond. Being your sire means I am here for you, *always*. You can talk to me about anything."

The moment I decide to tell him about the dark promise I made to Amicia, my throat closes. A knot so tight and thick forms, it prevents me from revealing my blood oath.

Misunderstanding my hesitation, Jasik continues. "I know you're angry with Amicia's decision, but is that all that's bothering you?"

Again, I try to tell him what Amicia made me do, but I swallow my words. Something inside me is screaming to speak, to admit my fault, to explain the blood oath, but in that same breath, something else squashes the desire. I'm torn between admitting the truth and dealing with the fallout and living in blissful ignorance. Maybe my concern is for nothing. Maybe a blood promise is common and there really is nothing to worry about.

"Ava?" Jasik squints, eyes concerned. Right about now, he's probably wishing he can read minds. I'm thankful he can't.

Finally finding my voice, I say, "I just hate to abandon Liv. It's not right. The cost of our feud shouldn't be her death."

Jasik exhales slowly, loudly, his eyes assessing me. "I agree."

He knows I'm hiding something. His gaze is piercing, as if he can see straight through to my soul. I gnaw on my lower lip, waiting for him to continue.

"But Amicia has made her decision," he says.

"And she speaks for all?" I ask, wondering how many others would have sided with me if they didn't fear her backlash.

Jasik nods. "As long as we are members of her nest, she does."

My heart sinks. Is this really how it will be from now on? If being a vampire means making enemies and helping those only deemed worthy by Amicia, then I want no part of this new life or my new family.

We haven't spoken since Jasik explained saving Liv is a lost cause. I'm angry with him for siding with Amicia over me. I wonder if he'd still care for his precious Amicia if he knew about the dark promise she forced me to make. Would he be upset knowing she basically cornered me and gave me no other option besides homelessness?

Every time I want to spill the beans about his fearless leader, something prevents me from speaking. I want him to feel my pain, my anger, but I don't want him to be mad at *me*.

I want to be wrong about Amicia. I want to believe her and trust in the blood oath. I want my home and family to be safe, but I can't fight the rising anguish that threatens to overwhelm me. I hate that I doubt her, but I can't help myself.

The deeper into the woods we travel, the more difficult the trek. I kick at a lush pile of snow with my military boots, and the tip of my shoe is dusted with fluff. The contrast between the stark white woodlands and my black hunting attire is jarring. Jasik is dressed to match, and I now understand why human hunters spend so much time in the apparel department. A rogue could spot us with very little effort.

The forest seems to travel for miles and miles, as if it has no end, but I know this isn't true. In fact, it ends rather abruptly where it touches Darkhaven. In one step, the world goes from endless rows of trees to a concrete slab, from nature to city in the blink of an eye.

I scan the trees, my gaze settling on the expansive wilderness. I see trees and more trees and even more trees in the distance. The air is cool and makes my skin tingle. I've learned this is how my senses distinguish different temperatures, because I'm essentially unaffected by them. I know it's cold, but I don't feel it. Walking the woods on this dark winter eve, I am content.

"It's snowing," Jasik says.

I glance at him. Just as I'm about to point out it's not snowing, a single flurry flutters before me and lands on my nose. I cross my eyes, trying to fixate on it. My vision blurs, eyes straining to focus on something so close and so small. I reach for the flake, accidentally squashing it with my fingertip.

I frown at my hand, where there is now a droplet of water. It's so small I almost can't see it. A human certainly couldn't. I turn to face Jasik, and the sky erupts. We are showered and coated in white. I laugh and brush off the snow that has covered Jasik's shoulders. He smiles when more covers the space I've just cleared.

Arms flanked out at my sides, I stare at the sky and spin in circles, watching as flakes drift all around me. Some small and some so large I can see their crystallized forms, they smack against my skin, sending a rush of vibrations down my spine at the startling sensation of being assaulted by something so weak.

Jasik stares at me, smiling widely as I enjoy the rush. A bolt of electricity surges through me at the charge from my heightened senses. The snow falls in a perfect swirling tornado of soft white bliss. The cold drops of shimmery ice speckle my face, sending goose bumps down my arms. I feel my skin prickle even under my jacket, and I shudder at the sensation. My nose is wet and pink, my lips dry and tight. But my heart is happy, and my pain is gone.

In these moments, when life seems so perfect, I forget clarity comes with a price. In Darkhaven, there is no such thing as peace.

I'm giggling, eyes wide with joy and heart racing from excitement, when we make eye contact.

Several yards away, he stands beside a tree. Blocked partially by a fallen branch, his form is obscured behind the brush, but I don't miss his eyes. One set of crimson irises that have an icy glow, laser-targeted right at me.

I'm running before Jasik even realizes what's happened. I hear him call out to me, shouting for me to stop, to wait, but inside, I'm burning. My magic is bubbling within my core, and it aches to be released.

FOUR

The snowfall is heavy. Unlike Jasik, I didn't sense the incoming storm, and I certainly didn't plan to hunt a rogue in the midst of a blizzard.

When I reach the tree, my prey is long gone. Having seen my approach, he must have retreated. The skin on the back of my neck tingles, and I turn, sure I'll see him watching me. I don't. I can barely see even a few feet in front of me. The thick, white blanket coating the earth is making it difficult even to track his footsteps.

I crouch, finding craters in the fresh snow, but the divots are quickly filled in. I curse and swipe my hand through it, smacking the fluff and sending it flying into a nearby bush.

Standing, I scan my surroundings. I consider shouting for Jasik, who should have reached my side by now, but I don't. I can't let the rogue know where I am. I take comfort knowing if I can't see him, he can't see me. I assume this is why Jasik hasn't called for me since I left him behind to chase a rogue vampire.

I was careless. Hunting without a plan is never wise, but by now, Jasik is used to my recklessness in battle. I think with my heart, running steadfast into the dangerous unknown. My carelessness has gotten worse since I transitioned into a vampire, but I have yet to die. So I must be doing something right.

I trudge through the snow, the piles quickly reaching the top of my boots. My jeans are tucked into them, preventing the crystallized water from icing my already-cold skin.

My T-shirt is wet from being pelted by the snow, so I zip up my jacket. My heart sinks, mind numb to the realization. Normally, I wouldn't ever do this. My jacket's inner pocket is where I kept my stake. I needed it to be one quick swipe away from killing a vampire, and having to unzip my jacket would take far too much time.

But I don't have to worry about that anymore. Mamá stole the weapon Papá gave me, and I doubt she'll ever return it. For my remaining years as a hunter of rogue vampires, I will fight with someone else's weapon. I feel like I betrayed my stake by being so careless with it. Regardless of what happened that night, I shouldn't have been so distracted that I left it behind.

I hear something behind me, and I spin around to face my attacker—except I'm alone. No one is there. Again, I hear a noise, and I spin to face it. Over and over again, I spin, certain I will come face-to-face with the rogue who occupies these woods.

Spinning 'round and 'round, I'm lost. The world is blinding white. I can't see anything but the constant assault of snowflakes peppering my face. My skin is slick—from nerves or the snow or both, I'm not sure—and I push back hair that clings to my moist forehead.

I fall to my knees. My heart is racing, my thoughts jumbled. My chest heaves and burns as I struggle to sift through the endless landscape before me. Hacking, I take in too much air. My overstretched lungs ache. I feel myself on the verge of a panic attack, so I try to calm myself, ignoring the danger lurking behind the sheets of snow encasing me. I may not be alone, but I certainly *feel* alone.

"You're fine, Ava," I whisper.

The back of my neck feels hot and sticky. I swipe my hand over the skin, rubbing my cold fingers against burning flesh to cool down. I scoop a pile of snow and press it to my neck. This works far better than my sleek, icy fingers.

My mouth is dry. I try to lick my lips, but my tongue sticks to the chapped skin. On my hands and knees, I stare at the ground. The snow is growing deeper with each passing second. My arms sink into its depths, and my wrists are no longer visible. Unable to see the ground or my own two hands, I feel as though I've been swallowed whole. I'm in the belly of the beast, and as I look around, I see no way out.

"You're going to be *okay*," I say.

This time, I speak more forcibly, and I catch the attention of the rogue. This time, I know I hear his approach. The earth shakes as he charges toward me. The echo of crushed snow is carried to my ears by the dry, lifeless air.

I feel his eyes burning into the back of my head, and I shoot to my feet and turn to face him.

We collide. The force of his body thrust against mine sends me falling backward. I sink into the snow, my head thrashing against the frozen ground. Stars dance behind my eyes when I make impact with the tundra.

Sweat drips into my eyes, and they sting. I blink away the salty fluid and stare up at him. His empty crimson irises shine brightly above me, a jarring contrast to the blinding white abyss we're inhabiting. We're secluded in a vortex, torn from the rest of the world.

The rogue smiles at me, his teeth almost as bright and white as the snowy prison we're trapped in.

He says something, but I don't hear him. I'm distracted by the howling wind that sends freshly planted snow up from the ground to cover my face. I shake it away, but more trickles back. It coats me, and I'm overwhelmed by the eerie sensation of being buried alive. Frozen in place, I'm queasy as the rogue smiles down at me as if he can read my thoughts.

The rogue says something again. My face must betray my inability to understand him, because his eyes are amused with me.

He digs his fingers into my arms, pinning me in place. I wince as he bruises my flesh, but he does not draw blood. He's holding back ... Why?

"You aren't my first," the rogue says loudly. The roar of the storm ceases long enough for me to hear his confession.

I hear him, but I still don't understand his words. His first what? Victim? Vampire kill?

Believing he's stalling as some sort of torture technique, I struggle against him. He budges slightly, but his strength barely wavers. I can't pull my arms free. I wiggle my wrists, digging my fingers into the compacted earth. Frozen snow digs under my fingernails, and I squirm at having something so cold in a place never meant to be bared. My skin is sensitive to the assault, and an itchy sensation rises up my arm, settling in my chest.

I groan and grumble, howl and bellow, hoping Jasik will hear the attack. I shriek for him, but I'm silenced when the rogue speaks again.

"And you make three," the rogue says. He emphasizes each word, pausing briefly after each breath.

Suddenly, he's lowering himself onto me. Fangs bared and saliva dripping onto my jacket, he slumps down as he pierces my neck. I screech at the impact of his fangs tearing through my flesh.

I jerk from side to side, hoping to whack him with my skull or jab him with my shoulder. Almost as soon as it began, it's over, and the rogue is off me.

I scramble to my feet, clutching my wound. Already, my skin begins to heal. The snow at my feet is stained with crimson, a jolting revelation of just how much blood I lost. I stumble as I stand, woozy from moving too quickly after a harrowing attack.

A screech pierces the silent night. It takes several blinks for me to realize the sound is coming from the rogue. He's screaming, clutching his throat. I glance around for Jasik, but my enemy and I are alone. If Jasik didn't pull this beast off me, then how was I freed?

I see it as my attacker moves, thrashing about. The pain must be unbearable. With balled fists, the rogue slams his hands into the earth—once, twice, three times. He bellows with agony and tears at his chest, shredding his shirt. His skin is bared to me, and I cringe at the sight.

Our gazes meet briefly; his eyes betray not only his agony but also his confusion. He's just as lost as I am.

"Wh-What have y-you done to me?" the rogue stutters behind a clenched jaw.

I trudge toward him, pushing through the snow to reach his side. My chest is heaving as my nerves begin to settle. My wound has healed, the blood at my neck slowly freezing. Later, it will be caked to my skin, and I'll have to scratch it off in the shower.

I lower the zipper of my jacket only an inch or so and let my cross drop freely. In our struggle, it must have poked through enough to touch the rogue, because his skin is tainted by burns. Cratering into his flesh, the cross branded him deeply.

What's more shocking than this rogue vampire cowering before me as he clutches his wounded throat is his eyes. He is not surprised by the revelation that I, a *vampire*, can touch a cross. I hold it in my hand, running my stiff fingers over the cool, silver metal. When I tuck it back inside my jacket, I make sure to place it beneath my T-shirt so the rogue can see it's gracing my skin. Still, his eyes do not waver.

I drop to my knees beside him. He cringes, grunting fiercely as something eats away at his tissue. The cross affected Jasik too, but not like this. This wound spreads, viciously tearing through the rogue's skin. It's as if the cross knows true evil, and it's banishing this demon straight to hell.

"What did you mean?" I say from my knees beside him. I don't fear for my safety. He can barely contain his own pain; he doesn't have the strength to inflict more on me.

He howls as his wound deepens. Soon, I'll see bone. If I want answers, I need to act fast.

"You said I make three. What does that mean?"

Someone approaches, and I jerk my head to find Jasik approaching. Coated in white, he races to my side, sliding to his knees and withdrawing his dagger. Just as he plunges it toward his victim, I grab on to his wrist, stopping Jasik from killing the rogue. Confusion flashes in his eyes, but he withdraws his weapon.

"You're okay?" Jasik asks. He fingers my jawline before brushing hair from my eyes. His gaze drops to my neck, and he freezes. Anger flashes behind his crimson irises, and I know I have only seconds to convince him to let the rogue live—*for now*.

"I'm fine," I say.

I return my attention to the rogue vampire, hoping Jasik will understand why I stopped him, why I *need* the rogue to respond.

"Answer me," I order.

The rogue grumbles under his breath, an inaudible confession that flares my frustration to life. He's wasting time, and unfortunately, time is a luxury he no longer has. If he won't willingly explain himself, I will force him to. With only moments before his inevitable demise, I make a rash decision.

In a swift motion, I pull the dagger from Jasik's hand and plunge it into the rogue's chest. I miss his heart—intentionally.

"Either you can make this harder than it needs to be, or I can make your pain go away," I say. "Your choice."

"Ava," Jasik says, his voice soft but pointed. He places his hand over mine, and I dare a peek at him. Before his eyes become unreadable, I see the flash of disgust in them. "We don't torture rogues. That would make us no better than them."

I understand what he's saying, and he's right. We fight to rid the world of evil, and if we resorted to torturing rogues for information, we would be no better than the monsters we slay. In my heart and even in my mind, I know this to be true, but my mouth and my hand have their own plans. I'm simply a bystander in their crusade. I face the rogue, ignoring Jasik's plea.

"I said, what did you mean?" I twist the knife in his chest, nicking bone. The rogue cries out and hacks up blood. I've just shortened his life by several more minutes.

"You're not the only one," the rogue shouts. "I've fought others like you."

Jasik's breath hitches, and I don't miss it. His shock fuels my desire to know more, to learn the truth once and for all.

"What do you mean, there are more? More what?" I'm shouting, my voice screechy. With sloppy hair frozen to my forehead and disheveled clothes, I'm sure I look like a crazy person right now. I imagine my eyes are wide and hungry, betraying my own inner demons.

"*Half-breeds*," the rogue whispers. He squeezes his eyes shut as tiny red lines spider-web from the center of his wound through his torso. I bet he hasn't been this close to death since the day he transitioned.

"You've met more witches who were turned?" I clarify. "How many? Where? Who? Did you kill them?"

A million questions are racing through my mind, but the rogue doesn't answer any of them, because in one swift motion, Jasik reclaims his dagger and plunges it into the vampire's heart.

I scream as the rogue combusts. The pristine snow is stained gray, tainted by his ash. In a second that passes far too quickly, the rogue is gone—and so are my answers.

I stare at my sire, my mouth wide with shock, with disdain, with *fear*. Jasik offered this rogue far greater leniency than he ever deserved. This monster never knew or showed such compassion, and now I'll never know the truth.

Once again, I'm left in the dark, but this time, I'm forced into seclusion by my own savior.

By the time we return to the manor, the silence between us is deafening. Not only have I refused to speak with Jasik, but he also hasn't even tried to look at me.

Lost in thought, I kick off my boots as I enter the foyer. Jasik slams the door behind us, jolting several nearby vampires. They retreat from the ensuing fury by taking the stairs in the sitting room to the second story.

It's unnaturally hot in the manor, and the snow at my feet is beginning to melt. I try to soak up the pooled water with my sock, only succeeding in swishing around what my sock can't absorb. Now a sopping mess, my socks cling to my feet and squish between my toes. I grimace. There are few things more uncomfortable than wearing wet socks.

"Everything okay?" Malik says. I look up from my feet to see him approaching. He's wearing lounge jogger pants and is holding a book. He snaps it closed when he sees our faces and sets it on a nearby bookshelf. It looks just as out of place as I feel.

"Gather everyone. We need to talk," Jasik says. He pushes past his brother, leaving me behind as he enters the parlor and plops onto a chair directly to the right of the fireplace.

While we were out, someone started a fire, and a pile of logs is stacked in the corner of the room. The earthy musk of freshly chopped wood is overwhelming, but not as much as the sounds, smell, and heat coming from the fireplace. The second I step into the room, I'm struck by a heat wave so fierce, it steals the breath from my chest.

It doesn't take long for the other hunters to meet us in the parlor. Even Holland joins us. I smile at Jeremiah's ex-boyfriend. In a room full of worried vampires, Holland is the only friendly face. I wonder if the fact that he's a witch affects my judgment. After all, the vampires seem to think I'm blinded by those deemed magical.

"What happened?" Hikari asks the moment she enters

the room, Jeremiah trailing behind her. She finds her way to an open seat and plops down, all the while staring at me. She's waiting for me to break, but Jasik called this meeting. I'll let him speak first.

"Is it the witches?" Jeremiah asks. I watch as Holland physically winces. His ex has such disdain for everything he is, and that breaks my heart.

"No," Jasik says simply.

"Then what is it?" Amicia asks.

Our leader enters the room, eyes narrowed. I don't have to be a mind reader to know she believes I told Jasik about the blood oath. My throat tightens as she approaches me. Of all the empty seats, she chooses to sit directly beside me. We share a couch far too small for two people, and our bodies touch. Once again, being this close to her sends a shudder through me. It makes me physically ache to be near her, and I don't know if it's because she's threateningly powerful or because of what she made me do.

"We encountered a rogue," Jasik explains.

Amicia straightens, her interest piqued. Now that she understands I didn't break her trust, the tension in my shoulders loosens, and I sit back against the couch. I can breathe again.

"From the same nest?" Amicia asks.

I shake my head. "I don't think so. I've never seen him before."

"That doesn't mean he wasn't part of that nest," Malik counters.

"Your former coven hasn't met everyone from ours," Hikari explains. "That doesn't mean there aren't more besides us."

"But this was different," I say. "He wasn't holding a grudge like the others. I'm not sure he even knows there was a rogue nest in Darkhaven."

"He was there for *you*, Ava," Jasik says.

I'm not sure how to take this. Is he agreeing with the others? Is he siding with me? If Jasik believes the rogue was there for me, then he must also believe that there are more creatures like me out there somewhere, just like the rogue said. After all, that's why he came—to see me, to find me. But in the woods, Jasik was sure he was lying. What changed?

When I finally break eye contact with my sire, I glance around the room. It's eerily silent, all eyes on me. I choke on my breath and cough to clear my throat.

"Not in the same way," I say softly.

"What's going on?" Jeremiah says, eyeing us curiously.

I'm not surprised we seem . . . off. Jasik and I can usually morph into the same being in times of duress. We're usually so in sync with each other, but lately . . . things have been different between us. Every time we take a step forward, something happens to bring us to a screeching halt, or worse—to force us back several paces.

"The rogue told Ava she isn't the only hybrid he's met," Jasik says plainly.

The room erupts in gasps, and I frown at Jasik. Why is he so bothered by this? He's been acting strange ever since he killed the rogue. He seems . . . *angry*. Is he mad at me because of how I acted, or is he upset with the rogue for telling me the truth?

"You can't possibly believe him," Amicia says.

I arch a brow as I tear my gaze from Jasik. "Of course I believe him."

"Ava, this does seem . . . weird," Hikari says.

"It's been months. Don't you think we would have heard about other half-breeds by now?" Jeremiah cuts in.

"He was lying to you," Jasik says. His eyes are emotionless, and it shakes me to my core. Jasik has never been so matter-of- fact.

"Why? What's the point? He was already dead," I say, crossing my arms over my chest. How am I the only one who believes him? I glance at Holland, who seems lost in thought. He doesn't meet my gaze. I wonder if he knows anything. After all, he is a witch.

"Maybe he was trying to distract you or something?" Jeremiah adds.

"That wouldn't surprise me," Malik agrees. "Rogues are notoriously untrustworthy."

"No, it didn't happen that way. He was too far gone. I used my cross necklace to get away, and it . . ." I trail off. How can I explain what it did? These vampires know the damage a cross inflicts, but have they ever seen it used against a rogue? It was nothing like what happened to Jasik. It was *brutal*.

"It burned him." Malik tries to finish my sentence for me, but *burn* isn't the proper word for what my cross did to that rogue vampire.

I shake my head. "It incinerated his skin. It branded him so viciously, it actually spread. In the end, tiny red veins flushed through his chest like spider webs. It didn't just mark him; it *tortured* him. It's almost as if the cross could sense how evil and soulless a creature he was, and it inflicted worse damage because of it."

Once again, the room is silent. I eye Jasik, wondering if he will expose my misdeeds. I shouldn't have tortured the rogue, even if he did deserve it. My job is to protect the innocent, not punish the guilty. Quick, abrupt attacks are what I'm trained to do. I'm not meant to prolong the pain like some psychopath. But I don't regret what I did, and that makes dealing with the aftermath so much worse.

"I've never used a cross in my dealings, so I'm unfamiliar with how it affects rogues differently than other vampires," Amicia says. Her voice is even, but I would guess her mind is reeling at this new information. If there was a way to harness the power of the cross, the vampires would be unbeatable. At her core, Amicia is a leader. She knows no other way than to protect her vampires.

"It makes sense, though," Holland says, his voice soft, squeaky.

"Hmm?" Jeremiah says. He leans forward, eyes on his ex.

Holland clears his throat before continuing. "I mean, what Ava said. That makes sense. If you consider the cross an ally to mortals, then on a scale of good to evil, rogues are just one step away from being the devil himself."

"I wonder what would happen if a rogue stepped inside a church," Hikari says.

"That would be interesting," Holland agrees.

"Let's not get carried away," Amicia says to the others before looking at me. "Ava, I know you're upset about the events earlier today, and now this rogue has given you hope that you're not truly alone, but I need you to see that that's all this is. You're scared of an eternity of alienation, but you mustn't believe his lies."

I exhale sharply. Part of what Amicia says is true. I don't want to face forever alone, but until this very second, I didn't *feel* alone. I knew I had Jasik and Malik and the others on my side. Amicia has a strange way with her words. In the same breath, she can both comfort and divide.

"In all my years, I have *never* met a creature quite like you," Amicia continues.

"Neither have I," Malik adds.

"I know you want to believe him, Ava, but he lied to you," Jasik says.

"Why would he do that?" I ask. That rogue might have been a lot of things, but I'm not sure a liar is one of them.

"For kicks and giggles?" Jeremiah says. "I mean, if not to free himself, then I'd guess he did it for his own enjoyment."

"I mean, look at you," Hikari says. "He's gone. He is *never* coming back, yet here you are, tormented by his words. And how long will you let yourself feel this way? He's doing exactly what he planned to do. He might have experienced seconds of unbearable pain, but you're willingly walking into an eternity of self-torture."

The room falls silent, leaving me with nothing but my own thoughts. As confusing as it is and as mixed up as I feel, I do believe them. I do think a rogue would lie to save himself, but I also saw his eyes when he spoke. Nothing about him made me feel like he was being dishonest. Even if the gamble was small, that minor chance mattered. Because if he *wasn't* lying, that can only mean one thing.

He was telling the truth.

I am not alone.

FIVE

The subtle ticks from the hallway grandfather clock lull me to sleep. The steady swoosh from my overhead ceiling fan makes my skin prickle.

I'm standing beside my bed—a massive four-poster throne with a sweeping sheer enclosure—and staring at myself while I sleep.

The astral plane is finicky, always just out of reach for anyone not born a spirit witch. This was one of my many psychic gifts as a mortal, and luckily, I was able to keep my connection to the other plane even after death.

I rarely visit the astral plane willingly. Without anyone to visit, it's an ever-constant reminder of how lonely my life has become. The night I transitioned, I visited my old house, and Mamá was there. She tethered herself to my connection, and that was the last time she welcomed me with warmth and love. Since then, I barely recognize the woman she's become.

I imagine my transition to vampirism has been hard on her. Me—the granddaughter of *Abuela*, our coven's high priestess—a *vampire*. Sometimes I still can't believe how different things are now. My former existence both feels like a lifetime ago and like no time has passed at all.

I watch myself sleep, and I frown. Mamá isn't the only one who's changed. My skin is pale, my body toned. My frame is small but not frail. Even before I became a vampire, I would have considered myself a formidable opponent, but I wasn't. I relied too heavily on little things to win my battles.

I finger my cross necklace. I feel it beneath my grasp, but I know it's not there...because I'm not really here. Not physically, anyway. I visit the astral plane with my mind. Everything about it mirrors the physical plane, the one that truly exists and bears life.

The astral world is a chilling reminder of how fragile we are. Every living soul is one brutal mistake away from this eternal darkness—always close enough to touch but far enough from making actual contact.

I move the sheer drapes to better look at myself. I imagine this is what it would feel like to be a ghost, always haunting that which you cannot truly experience. I can't make contact with my physical self. When I reach to caress my cheek, my hand dissipates, flowing through my flesh, baring truth to the fact that this plane is nothing but barren, connectionless land. It mirrors its opposite plane in a desperate attempt to feel something, *anything.*

I consider roaming the manor, venturing into the other bedrooms to stalk my nestmates, but I know it would be pointless. They won't be there. Their beds will be vacant. I am the only spirit witch here tonight.

My physical form is here as a portal to the other world. It reminds me that I don't belong on the astral plane, and my body is my path home.

In the distance, the wind howls. With it, it carries the sound of a door closing. I jolt upright, backing away from my physical body. My spine tingles, and I shiver. It's an odd sensation. I have little to fear in this dreamscape. At any moment, my physical form can jostle awake, and I will be forced out.

Breath hitched, I listen to the house. It creaks, the noise dancing around my head. I tell myself it's just the wind. I look outside. The woods are eerily dark. Shadows loom, and clouds cover the moon. Everything seems gloomy and spooky. What few stars twinkle overhead illuminate the fresh snow. It glistens at me, and the juxtaposition between the beauty of the world and terror in my heart is nauseating.

I step away from the windows, contemplating leaving the astral plane. I should return to my body, waking safely in my own bed. I glance at myself sleeping. I look so peaceful, content, like my world isn't slowly crumbling all around me. With the news of other half-breeds, I've let myself forget about Liv. Even now, I try to shake away the memory of her. For all I know, she's already dead.

The hardwood floors groan in the distance, the distinct sound of old wood giving way under weight. I hear this noise almost daily. In a house full of vampires, someone is always walking around. But this is the astral plane, and I should be alone.

I tiptoe toward my bedroom door and place my ear against the wood. The solid oak seems impenetrable, but I close my eyes and listen. I wait for a second squeak, telling myself my mind is playing tricks on me.

The moment I hear it, I stumble backward, tripping over my feet and falling to my butt. The glow of the hallway light under my door is blinding in my dark bedroom. I stare at it, watching while listening as the steady squeak of approaching footsteps nearly chokes the life from me.

The footsteps grow louder with each passing second, and I'm immobilized by my fear. My heart is racing, chest heaving, and eyes wide with terror. A shadow moves, the light flickering across my bedroom floor. Darkness penetrates the light, and I know I'm not alone. Someone is standing on the other side of my bedroom door.

The screech of nails grinding against the wood slithers through the walls. A shudder works its way through me, and I open my mouth to speak. But no sound escapes my lips.

Two hard, jolting knocks against my door send me to my feet, and I rush forward. With my hand grasping the knob, I hear a whispering echo resonate in my chest. It stops my heart and makes my knees buckle.

Quickly, I jerk open the door, prepared to catch my stalker off guard, but no one is there. The hallway is empty.

I peer outside, seeing nothing but a long hallway and an endless row of closed doors. I tiptoe toward the stairs and peer into the downstairs sitting room. It's vacant, but a chill rises in the air. Something is urging me to run back to my body, jump in, and scream until my physical mind awakens.

I cross my arms over my chest and tighten my grasp, holding myself closely. My sputtering heart is making it difficult to focus. From the bottom step, the dining room is at my left, the hallway to the foyer at my right, and an entrance to the solarium is straight ahead.

Gnawing on my lower lip, I fully descend the stairs and take several cautious steps forward. I glance into the parlor, finding it as empty as the hallway upstairs. I walk the length of the solarium. It's vacant too.

When I reach the dining room, I freeze. The kitchen light is on. It glows beneath the swinging door. When I reach the butler's pantry, which connects the kitchen and dining room, I stop short of pushing open the door. Instead, I mentally prepare myself for what may be inside.

My imagination is wild, and I envision so many different monsters beyond this door. The realist in me chastises the child, because I *know* I have to be alone here. The astral plane is home to spirits—nothing else.

I glance out the window, peering into the backyard. The trees surrounding our property seem to take on new forms. They turn into monsters with stark, sharp arms and wild-flowing hair. They tower over me, their shadows looming ever closer.

I squeeze my eyes shut until it hurts my head. When I open them again, the monsters are gone, leaving only trees.

My throat is closing in on itself, and I choke out a breath. With my attention back on the kitchen, I gnaw my lower lip until it bleeds. It stings as I tongue the droplets of blood.

The squeaking floor suddenly stops, as if my intruder is aware of my arrival. Time seems to slow as I stare at the door, waiting for something—*anything*—to happen. After several agonizing seconds, I find the strength to enter the kitchen.

I push open the door with such force it slams against the wall. Shaking, I stare into his eyes. He's smiling, a deviant glare to his crimson irises.

"I was wondering how long it would take you to find me in here," he says. His accent is thick, but I cannot place it.

Goose bumps prickle on my exposed arms, and I'm suddenly aware that I'm wearing pajamas. A too-sheer-for-comfort nightgown that flows against my frame each time I move.

My intruder is dressed in jeans, a dark T-shirt, and a jacket. When the microwave beeps, his floppy, curly brown hair sways as he turns around. When he faces me again, I've managed to take a few more steps toward him, and he's holding a mug. My stomach pangs as the smell of freshly nuked blood wafts my way.

I lick my lips, daring a peek at his steaming drink, before our gazes meet again. His eyes are amused with me, and he holds out his breakfast, offering it to me. I shake my head, not stupid enough to drink something I didn't make myself.

I was under the impression that I couldn't be hurt while visiting the astral plane, so sustenance here should do nothing for my physical form. But I also believed I could only be visited by spirit witches, yet I stare into the eyes of a vampire. I'm beginning to wonder if everything I was taught before my transition was a lie.

"We don't have much time," he says.

His statement is a bit too ominous for my liking, so I take a few steps back until I'm safely beneath the doorframe. I make mental calculations, assuming I can outrun him to my body if needed.

In this form, I don't have access to my vampire strength. After all, I'm nothing but a wisp. That should mean he doesn't have access either. That is, if we're playing fair, but I've never come across a fair playing field in Darkhaven.

"I'm not going to hurt you," he says, and then he takes a long, sloppy sip from his mug. I cringe as he slurps down blood, the sound radiating off my bones.

"Who are you?" I ask, voice cracking. I hate that I sound so nervous, so scared. I shouldn't be afraid of him. He's in *my* house.

"Will," he says simply. He arches a brow as he takes another slurp of blood. When he sets down his mug, his teeth are stained pink.

"What are you doing here?" I ask, my voice harder than before. Maybe I sound more courageous than I feel right now, and that's a good thing. I don't want him to know how terrified I am of the fact that *he* is in *my* astral visit.

"Looking for you," Will says. He smiles, eyes glimmering in the low lighting.

My breath hitches. So he did come for me. What does that mean? If he wanted to hurt me, wouldn't he have tried to already? If he can find my astral self, then surely he knows where my physical body is too.

"What was with the show earlier?" I ask, remembering the scratches at my door and the dancing light beneath it.

A sly grin creeps its way onto his face. "I wasn't sure I could find you, and when I did, I thought I'd play a little game. After all, you only have one first encounter. I wanted ours to be memorable."

"So you thought terrifying me was the way to go?" I don't hide my annoyance. "How are you even here right now?"

While I wait for his answer, I think about the one question I *should* be asking: *why* was he looking for me? But I can't ask that—not now. I'm worried his answer will be worse than our encounter.

"I admit it was in poor taste. I shouldn't have scared you, but can you blame me?" Will says, laughing it off. He takes another sip of blood.

"Yes," I say. I'm not sure why he's even eating. Nothing in the astral plane is real, so that blood is providing no nourishment. It's all an act—and he's putting on a show for me. But why?

"So who are you?" I ask.

"I'm someone who likes to track *special* vampires—ones like you."

A knot forms in my throat. I suppose I shouldn't be surprised that he knows I'm different. Clearly I'm a witch. I mean, I'm in the astral plane, but my irises are crimson. He can tell I'm not *just* a witch.

"Why?" I ask. "And how did you get here?"

What do you want with me?

He attempts to take another sip of blood, but the mug disappears before it touches his lips. He frowns, gaze flickering from his hand to me.

"You're waking up," he says plainly.

"No," I say, shaking my head. I'm not talking to him; I'm speaking to my physical self, the one that's asleep in my bed. I need to convince myself not to wake up, if that's even possible. I'm not ready to leave Will. I have too many unanswered questions. He can't leave yet.

"Sadly, yes," he says.

I blink, and he's in front of me. He moved so fast, I didn't even see the motion. One second he was by the microwave, and the next he was beside me.

I shriek and fall backward, moving so quickly my feet skid against the hardwood floor. My knees lock, and I'm falling. Only, I never reach the ground. Will snaps his arms forward, grabbing my wrists. He holds me firmly and pulls me toward him. The space between us is gone, and I feel his breath hot against my skin.

I shiver beneath his hard, cold gaze, my legs numb beneath me. If he were to let go, I would collapse to the ground in a sloppy heap.

He smiles, but something is off about it. It's menacing, and his eyes glow.

I shake my head, unwilling to leave but not wanting to stay.

"Just tell me what you want," I whisper.

"You."

I shake, trying to pull away from him. He releases me, and I dash through the dining room, not looking back. I don't listen for his footsteps because I don't want to know how close he is to reaching me. I just need to make it to my body. I can sever my connection there, and I can leave the astral plane behind and never return.

"You can't run away from me, Ava," Will shouts. "I already found you. I know where you are."

I take the steps two at a time, stumbling when I reach the top. I shimmy down the hall on my hands and knees until I find the strength to stand again.

When I reach my door, my palms are slick from sweat, and I hear him stomping up the stairs. I scream, wiping my hands on my nightgown, and slam my body against the door. It doesn't budge, so I hit it again. By the time it finally opens, I see Will rounding the corner.

He shouts something at me just as I fall into my bedroom. I'm only feet away now.

I can do this. I can make it.

I crawl to my bed and rip through the sheer fabric enclosing my body. I shred lace, tearing through the web of mesh. It lands in heaps at my feet.

When I finally reach my body, I can see that my physical form is restless. Slowly, I am waking, and when I do, this will feel like a nightmare. I will have to convince myself it wasn't. This is something *more*.

Will is standing in my doorway. The light from the hall glows around him, casting eerie shadows across his features. His face is dark, but I can see his smile, his glowing eyes.

I scream and grab on to my body.

"Wait. Don't—"

.I jolt awake, eyelids snapping open so quickly my head hurts. I sit up in bed, chest heaving, and stare into my dark, quiet bedroom. My pulse is racing, my bed soaked from sweat.

Suddenly someone is at my door. The loud echoes of harsh knocking radiate off the walls. Before I can slip from the bed, Jasik is entering.

"Are you okay?" he asks, but he doesn't wait for me to respond. He's scanning the room, checking my closet and bathroom for monsters that hide in the shadows.

My throat is closing, and I cannot answer him. But I nod.

His gaze settles on me. "You're shaking."

"I'm okay," I whisper.

As I reach for my blankets that lie in a bundle on the floor, I notice the marks on my wrists. I stare, gaze tracing each delicate curve of both handprints.

"What is it?" Jasik asks. Slowly, he walks toward me.

"Do you see them?" I ask. I can't look away. I worry if I do, they'll disappear.

Jasik doesn't answer. Instead, he turns on the bedroom light, and a blinding flash illuminates the room.

But the moment the shadows retreat, the marks are gone. Still, I can't help but feel like they really were there, and if they were, my dream wasn't simply a nightmare.

It was a warning.

SIX

The basement training quarters are suffocating. The room itself is airy and large, with cushiony mat floors, a wall of mirrors, and a long table housing various weapons to wield. But there's something stagnant in the air. The smell of impending doom is formidable, and it tastes like raw sewage.

Today, I wear a breezy two-piece. The spandex shorts and sports bra allow me to watch the way my body moves during training. I'm convinced there is a connection between my vampire senses and the magic inside me, but today I'm distracted. I can't focus long enough to dodge Malik's attacks, and his frustration is evident. He's already chastised me once. I can see he's again at his boiling point.

"Ava, I know you're upset about Amicia's decision, but you need to focus."

I frown, looking up at him from where I lie on the floor. The mats are soft beneath me, and I burrow my elbows into the mush, pretending I can escape this place and Malik's accusations.

He stares at me, a funny grimace on his usually pristine face. "What is it?"

"I'm not upset with Amicia because of her decision. I understand why she doesn't want to help the witches." I grunt as I shuffle to my feet, dusting off my thighs instinctively. My hands are slick from my exertion. Malik certainly isn't holding back today.

"Then what's the problem? Our sessions are useless if you can't focus," Malik asks. His eyes are hard, his tone sharp, but I know he's not mad at me.

How can I answer this question? Sure, Amicia's decision *bothered* me, but that's not why I'm distracted. I can't stop thinking about my dream, wondering if my blood promise to Amicia is why I now have a dark shadow cast over me. There is no doubt in my mind that last night's nightmare is somehow connected to what we did.

The gnawing sensation in the pit of my gut is telling me to confide in Malik, even though I'm overwhelmed by sheer terror at the thought of betraying Amicia's confidence. She never explicitly stated not to tell anyone about the oath, but I'm pretty sure it was implied. Everything about it felt... *wrong*. That usually means I'm supposed to keep my lips sealed.

"We don't have a lot of time, Ava. Holland will be here soon to begin your magic training," Malik says, eyeing the clock on the wall.

My heart leaps at the thought of training with Holland. Today, we're focusing on calling the elements—something I used to do so easily when I was just a witch. I haven't tried to summon my magic that way since I turned, and I'm honestly not sure it will work. But the itching feeling crawling across my skin comes with a burning realization: I need to protect myself from whatever is coming. I woke with the stark realization that last night's nightmare was a warning, and I won't sit idly by while my life crumbles around me. It's time I fight back.

"I'm glad training with Holland brings you such joy," Malik says, voice deadpan.

My smile falls. "I'm sorry... You know I enjoy our sessions too, right?"

"Just tell me what's on your mind," he continues, waving away my concern.

"It's—It's probably nothing," I say, trying to convince myself more than Malik.

I want to tell him, but I'm suddenly struck with the notion that telling my trainer before I tell my sire could prove problematic. Even so, it feels easier to admit wrongdoing to Malik than to Jasik. He's like the older brother I never had and didn't know I wanted. Things with Jasik are complicated. One minute, I want to shout at him to kiss me already, and the next, we're fighting about ridiculous things. I definitely have better control over my emotions when I'm not in the same room as my sire.

"Great. That's exactly the kind of thing I want so overly distracting—absolutely *nothing* important." Once again, he feigns annoyance with me. I know Malik takes training seriously, but this might be a bit much. After all, do I even need combat training anymore? I'm pretty sure my rogue tally is much higher than anyone else's this week.

I chew on my lower lip, wincing when I nibble on raw flesh. I gather the strength to explain what happened when Amicia forced the vampires out of the house during our meeting. I inhale slowly, deeply, and exhale just the same. With each passing second, my muscles unclench. I stand straighter, taller, more confidently. And I know it's time.

"It's just..." I begin.

"Yes?" Malik arches a brow, both amused and concerned with my hesitation.

I sigh. "Amicia forced me to make a blood oath with her."

I spit out my words so quickly, they jumble together, but based on Malik's immediate reaction, I know he understood me just fine.

Every fiber of his body stiffens as my words settle over him. His eyes widen with shock, and his hands ball into hard fists at his sides. If it were possible, I would believe time actually slowed as he processed my words. He stares at me, unmoving and unblinking, like a monster on the brink of attack. He's looking at me, but I'm not so sure he *sees* me. His gaze is lost. But is he lost with my words, or has his mind been transported to another place completely?

"Malik?" I speak softly, hoping I don't jar him back to reality too harshly.

He blinks several times, his vision focusing on me again.

"She asked you to make a dark promise?" he asks, clarifying what I said earlier.

I nod. "She did."

"She shouldn't have forced you to do that." Malik's voice is hard and low, and I shiver. The coolness of his words settles into my bones, and I'm unsure I'll ever be able to shake the ice that now forms there. I wrap my arms around my chest, hoping to hold myself, to keep myself still, to keep my body warm.

Before I can muster the courage to ask him why this is so bad, Holland enters. With my back to the door, I don't see him, but I hear his approach. He whistles as he walks, a happy skip in his step.

Until it's gone.

The sudden halt of his stride is startling. I rush around, facing him. He eyes us curiously, unsure of how to proceed. His gaze scans my frame before darting to Malik.

"We were just finished here," Malik says. He sidesteps me

and exits the room before I can beg him to stay, to tell me what this means.

Why is Malik so concerned with the dark promise I made? What did Amicia make me do?

With Malik gone, the air in the room is heavy. I can't handle the accusations in Holland's eyes, so I turn away.

"What was that about?" Holland asks, but I'm already moving away from him.

"It was nothing," I say. Malik's immediate and tense reaction forces me to lie to Holland. I hate that the words spill so easily from my mouth. I don't want to lie to him—or to anyone, for that matter—but that uneasy sensation building in my stomach has me convinced I'll become quite good at lying by the end of the day.

"Is something going on between you two?" Holland asks.

His accusation halts me. I spin to face him, hoping the shock on my face is as evident as it is in my heart.

"Are you seriously asking me that?" I ask. Surprised by his words, I try to consider how things must appear to Holland as a bystander.

Holland shrugs. "This isn't the first time I've clearly interrupted something." His voice is emotionless, but his eyes silently judge me.

"Of course not. Malik is like a brother to me."

"Well, Malik *is* a brother to Jasik, so keep that in mind," he says, arms crossed.

"Holland, there is *nothing* happening here. I don't know what you think you saw, but Malik is just my trainer. He's a friend—nothing more."

I hope I don't look as tense as I feel. The last thing I want is for rumors to spread. I'm certain Jasik won't believe them, but things could get awkward between us. The other vampires won't take kindly to any rumblings of a tryst either.

"But you don't want to tell me what you were talking about?" Holland continues. "And why exactly did Malik rush out so quickly?"

"Training was over," I say.

He arches a brow, clearly not impressed with my explanation.

I sigh and opt for honesty. "Malik is concerned about something that happened between Amicia and me. It's nothing for you to worry about, okay?"

Holland relaxes, his arms dangling at his sides. He frowns and says, "Is everything all right?"

"It will be," I say, feigning confidence.

I give him my best smile—the one that's supposed to get me out of even the worst jams. He must accept it, because after several long seconds, he nods and changes the subject.

"So are you ready to summon the elements?" He smiles brightly, showing all of his polished, white teeth. He wiggles his brows, overly excited to test my limits once again. I wish I could fake such enthusiasm.

"I suppose..."

"What's the matter? Don't you want to see if you can?"

I nod. "I do, but... I'm just nervous."

And I have a lot *on my mind right now.*

"Don't worry about anything. I'm here. I'll reel you back in if it gets bad." Holland's voice is soft but confident. And I believe him.

"Just... don't let it get to that point, okay?"

He smiles. "Promise."

The silent hum of the house threatens to lull me to sleep. The soft patter of footsteps overhead reminds me that I'm not alone, even though the darkness of the room makes me feel like I am. With the lights off and without even a sliver of light to help illuminate the room, I can't see Holland. I hear him, though. I mimic his slow, deep inhalations and exaggerated exhalations. His breathing is comforting and eases my inner turmoil.

My arms are heavy. They rest atop my lap. I'm sitting cross-legged on the soft mat floor. My body sinks into it, the cushion giving way to my weight. I wiggle my toes and curl my fingers. Whenever I feel like I might drift away, I do this. It helps to ground my senses.

I breathe in deeply, slowly, until my lungs ache at the pressure, and then I exhale, releasing the tension in my shoulders.

I don't know how long we've been sitting here like this, but I know it's been far too long. It feels like days have stretched before us while we've secluded ourselves in this small space away from vampires and light.

Of course, I know this isn't true. It probably hasn't been even thirty minutes. That's the beauty of meditation. It allows me to escape this place, to release the negative energy even though I'm still securely planted in the midst of it.

The steady thump of my heart echoes in my mind. I envision the muscle pumping blood through my body, providing the fuel my magic needs.

I focus on that power. It swirls inside me, a bright, burning ball of shimmery, iridescent magic.

I tug at it, and it gives way to me. Slowly, it creeps from the depths of my soul and coats my skin, seeping out of my pores. It illuminates the room, sending a burst of light to every corner. A glistening sheen settles among us. Holland stares back at me, and I'm certain the excitement in his eyes matches my own.

I'm smiling so sincerely, it actually hurts my cheeks. A rush of giggles escapes my throat, and I don't try to push it down. I can't contain my excitement or the giddy feeling washing over me when I allow the magic inside to consume my entire body. I feel warm everywhere. No longer do I feel like I control the magic. All at once, *I* become the energy encased within it. With magic flowing all around me, it wraps around my body, covering me, protecting me, revitalizing me.

"I wish you could see it, Ava," Holland whispers. His eyes sparkle, and his hands are shaking.

I risk a peek at the wall of mirrors to my side, straining my neck until I can see what mesmerizes Holland.

The rush of energy all around me gives the glow of a physical appearance. It swirls and sparkles all around me, never straying too far. It illuminates the entire room and glimmers off my pale skin. I'm shiny and slick, strong and elated.

"Do you think you can summon a fireball?" Holland asks.

I face him, a sudden rush of nerves overpowering my initial excitement at practicing magic.

I swallow the knot in my throat and nod. "I'll try."

Closing my eyes, I focus on the fire element. I envision its strength and heat, its fury and dominance. As one of the strongest elements, it takes a powerful witch to maintain control over the element—and I imagine there is no stronger witch than one with the blood of a vampire.

Gnawing on my lower lip, I silently call to the element. I speak to it in my mind and in my heart, calling its name like I used to when I didn't survive on an all-liquid diet.

"Incendia."

The Latin word for fire rolls off my tongue with ease. It's familiar and makes me homesick. The feeling passes quickly, but it was there nonetheless. It leaves an emptiness—one I fear I'll never shake. The hollowness where my devotion to my coven once resided is a startling reminder that I can no longer rely on Mamá for guidance. If I want to control my magic, I need to learn to do so on my own.

I wait for the fire to thicken, but it doesn't. The air around me doesn't grow hot; my skin is not moist. There is no mist, no heat, no fire. There is only magic, and it coats my skin so tightly, I'm not sure where it ends and I begin.

I open my eyes, letting the vision of Holland before me blur.

"Incendia," I say again. My voice is soft, but my intention is powerful.

Still, nothing happens.

Defeated, I sigh, slouching over, relinquishing my hold on my magic. It dissipates, escaping back into my body, nestling itself inside. I sink into my hands, staring at the floor.

"Don't give up, Ava," Holland says. He shimmies toward me and rests his hand atop my own.

I look up at him. "I don't think this is going to work," I admit.

"Well, it won't with that attitude," he says pointedly.

I shake my head. "This just doesn't feel the same. This magic, whatever it is, *feels* different. It doesn't feel like one singular element."

Holland sits back, resting on his palms. With his arms outstretched behind him, he eyes me curiously, a funny look on his face. He's deep in thought, contemplating my predicament just like I should be.

"Maybe it isn't," Holland says.

"Isn't what?" I ask.

"Just one element."

SEVEN

I kick the snow at my feet, thinking about Holland's words. I should be focusing on patrolling the woods, especially since I'm hunting alone tonight. But I can't. Even the sounds of the forest have fallen mute. All I can hear are his words, and they loop endlessly in my mind.

Maybe it's not just one element.

I suppose that makes sense. After all, a spirit witch has access to all five elements, and maybe this magic is a culmination of them all. But what does that mean? What kind of power is that? What happens when all five elements blend into one power? Is this what happens when spirit becomes physical?

I sigh. There's still so much I don't know, don't understand. Will I ever have a handle on this new life? It seems like answers come with more questions.

I scan my surroundings, hoping to find a reasonable distraction, but the woods are devoid of life. It seems I'm the only restless soul out tonight.

I imagine the rest of Darkhaven is already lost in a deep sleep, and with the sun soon to rise, the vampires are finding their way home. I wasted too much time training with Malik and calling my magic with Holland. I should have hunted the moment the sun set. We've spent far too many hours pretending I'll get a handle on this, and I'm still no closer to understanding what's happening to me. Even though I try to convince myself otherwise, I feel like a lost cause.

I shake away the thought and reach for my cross necklace. It's cool to my touch. The silver metal sparkles, shimmering against my pale skin. I tuck it beneath my shirt, shivering as it cascades against my collarbone. Though I'm elated to know I can once again wear this cross, I know it comes at a price. To be worthy of its protection, I forfeited the one tool that gave me the confidence to vanquish whatever demons come my way.

I feel empty without my stake. It wasn't simply a weapon; it was an extension of my soul. Bound together with my magic, the silver metal tore through the flesh of my enemies. With it by my side, I never feared what lurked in the shadows. Now I'm surrounded by darkness, ever searching for my stake's guiding light.

I find myself walking closer to my former coven and farther from my new home. The vampires are busying themselves with their daily lives, and even without stalking them, I know the witches are struggling to find Liv. Stuck in the middle, I seem to be the only one out of place. I'm seeking guidance and finding silence.

Everyone has a plan, a place. Amicia says jump, and the vampires ask how high. She says we will not help the witches, and the vampires don't object. Meanwhile, I'm haunted so severely by my decision to forsake the witches, my regret is seeping into my dreams. I'm having nightmares that feel so real, I almost believe I should warn the others about the vampire I met.

I've been restless since I woke, a dark, ominous cloud hanging over me, threatening to clench the very life from my chest. The clouds hang low in the sky tonight, making it almost impossible to see clearly.

The air is heavy with mist, and it's snowing softly. The tiny, crystallized droplets are almost too small to see. They're more of an annoyance than anything else. The flakes cluster to my eyelashes and cling to my loose hair. I push away strands that have caked around my eyes and try to shake the feeling that I'm being watched.

"It's all in your head, Ava," I say aloud. I'm barely talking to myself at this point. I'm wasting time, fighting the inevitable. Going back to the manor means going to bed, and I'm not ready for that. I'm not ready to sleep. When I close my eyes, I see his, and I'm not prepared for another encounter.

Snow blankets the earth, sending a rush of energy through me. I don't feel the cold, but my mind knows no better. I remember what it was like to be human—to feel the cold, the heat. Strangely, my senses are heightened, but only in certain ways. In other ways, I'm hardened to the elements.

Maybe that's why I'm struggling to connect with my magic. If it is a culmination of spirit, which *is* the ultimate elemental control, then I need to harness what it means to be human, to be *mortal*.

I exhale slowly and then let a quick burst of air fill my lungs. Tapping into the elements seems like an easy task— after all, I'm surrounded by nature. Air is everywhere and in everything. With earth, I can create fire. With fire, I can melt snow into water. With the four elements accounted for, I turn to spirit.

I don't miss the irony in my most innate element causing me the most trouble. Before my transition, I enjoyed tapping into spirit. I would venture to the astral plane and relish in dreams of the future. Never once did I see my death or what awaits me after it claimed my soul. I didn't foresee losing my family or turning to the vampires for help.

Now when I think of spirit, I think of visions so terrifyingly real, I can barely close my eyes long enough to blink.

I kick at the ground, sending a spray of fresh snow cascading before me. It's not easy taking out my frustration on such a yielding subject. Sometimes I wonder if rogues are psychic. They always seem to avoid me during the hunts when I can really use a distraction.

Just as I consider turning back and calling it a night, something catches my attention. It's brief in time, a quick flash of danger that alerts my senses to his presence. He's too far to touch, but a sensation in my gut grows. It gnaws at me, warning me that I am not alone.

Something else is stalking these woods tonight.

I take a few steps closer, squinting through my frozen lashes. I need to draw closer, if only to ensure there really is cause to worry. Am I being hunted, or am I so distracted by my predicament that I can't think clearly?

The wind rustles dead brush, and with it, the howling sound of air scraping against wood permeates around me. It's distracting, and my gaze darts to the snow-covered mound before me.

Quickly, I leap over it, landing several feet on the other side. The moment my weight slams down, the ground grunts its protest. The crunch of snow radiates through my boots. My knees ache at the impact, and I run my fingertips along the snow as I crouch down.

I can feel him. The snow speaks to me, sending shock waves to my fingers every time he moves. The beauty of the elements is its connection. Everything meets, and with that connection, the world speaks to me as a hunter. It makes being a predator much easier, and on a night when the sun is soon to rise, I'll take every advantage I can get.

He jostles behind a tree, poking his head out from the shadows to find me. I've already spotted him. His crimson irises invite me in, and I smile.

I'm running before I've formed a plan, and I reach his side in record speed. I spin around the tree, hoping to catch him off guard, but the moment I loop around, he plants two fists firmly at my chest. I'm catapulted away, landing several feet from my intended target. Plopping squarely on my butt, I'm having training session flashbacks. Malik was right. I should have been focused today.

I stare up at him from where I sit, and my blood runs cold. A screech erupts from my chest but stops short of reaching my lips. Instead, I choke on it.

This isn't real. He can't be here!

"Hello, Ava," the vampire says.

"Will," I whisper, remembering his name from my earlier nightmare.

I jump to my heels, prepared to strike back, but he takes several steps backward, throwing his arms up in defense.

"I'm not here to hurt you," he says.

Unbelieving, I quickly withdraw my weapon—a simple dagger with a black-threaded handle—and slice it through the air between us. I want him to know I'm familiar with this weapon, even if it's not my trusty stake, and fully prepared to end his life if needed. I may be absolutely terrified right now, but if only one of us is making it home tonight, I'll make sure it's me.

"Don't you think I would have attacked by now if I wanted to hurt you?" he asks. "I've been following you for at least an hour."

I inhale sharply. *That long?*

"Yes, that long," Will says with a smile. I hate that he knows me this well. I've never been good at hiding my emotions, and I never cared when my family knew what I was thinking without me speaking my mind. But it's different when my enemy uses this against me. He shouldn't know what I'm thinking or how I'm feeling.

"What are you doing here? What do you want with me?" I shout, maintaining my hold over my weapon. I refuse to lower it—not until I feel safe enough to turn my back on him. And I don't foresee that happening anytime soon.

"I came looking for you," he says. "I thought I made that fairly clear." He makes a pointed face, and it irritates me.

"What do you want with me?" I ask, afraid of his honesty. A new vampire has come to town vying for my attention. And he has it.

A thought occurs to me. This vampire has made it pretty clear that he's been hunting me—and not just tonight. He found a way into my dreams, into the astral plane. Will just happens to find me in Darkhaven, and my former best friend goes missing? If I've learned nothing else from becoming a vampire, I have learned there is no such thing as coincidences.

I decide to be direct. I haven't the time for dishonesty. "What have you done with Liv?"

He arches a brow, a confident glow of confusion crossing his face. "Who?"

"Liv. Where is she?" I ask, repeating myself.

My voice is forceful. I need him to believe he's made some

mistake. We can do this one of two ways: the easy way or the hard way. If he believes I know more than I do, he might just admit his wrongdoing, and there might be enough time to save her.

He frowns, his floppy brown hair blowing when the breeze picks up. His skin is pale, his eyes two glowing red rubies. His polished skin creases where his forehead betrays his concern.

"I have no idea who that is. I'm here for *you*." He adjusts the lapels of his jacket, a cocky confidence in his demeanor that makes my blood boil.

"So I'm supposed to believe it's a coincidence that you come to town the very day she goes missing?"

"Liv is missing?" he asks, both clarifying my accusation and confusing me in the same breath.

"I— Yes, she's missing." I relax, my shoulders in knots. His confusion is settling over me, and I'm starting to believe he really didn't have anything to do with her disappearance, which means there's yet another vampire in town looking for payback. Will this ever end?

"Who is she?" Will asks.

"She is . . . *was* . . . my best friend."

Will sucks air through his teeth, and the hissing noise splits my brain. "Sounds like things ended badly."

"Well, you know . . . vampire now," I say, pointing at my core as if that's where my vampire powers reside, as if my situation is not painfully obvious by my crimson irises, fangs, and pale skin.

"Ah, now we're getting to the juicy stuff," Will says. "Liv is a witch."

I hesitate before answering but ultimately confirm. After all, he says he's been looking for me, for *special vampires*, so he must know that I was once not only mortal but a *witch*.

He nods. "I can see how you might think I am responsible for her disappearance, but trust me, I'm only here for you."

"That really doesn't make me feel better about this situation," I admit.

He laughs. "I suspect it doesn't."

"Who are you?" I ask, utterly confused by our total encounter.

He smiles. "Well, I could *tell* you, or I could *show* you..."

I don't respond, so he must take my silence as my willingness to continue this odd exchange. I hate to admit that I might have been wrong about him. He truly doesn't seem interested in harming me, which only leaves one question.

What does Will want with me?

He answers my question without even speaking.

With the flick of his wrist, a fireball sparks to life, floating within his grasp but never fully touching his skin. He bounces it a little, toying with the scorching heat that's mere feet before me. With one quick snap, he could end my life, yet I don't feel threatened. In fact, I feel so completely mesmerized by his magic trick, I'm walking toward him, as if my legs are powered by my emotions, not by my brain.

When I've closed the space between us, I reach for the small ball of fire, running my fingertips along its edge. I'm not confident enough to actually touch it, but I need to *feel* it. I don't feel the heat of the flame, but I do feel the power of his magic. I've only felt this kind of raw, pure strength from one other vampire: Amicia.

I tear my gaze from the fireball and glance up at Will. He's smiling down at me. The space between us is almost nonexistent. I didn't realize how close we became, but now that I'm just a breath from his skin, I'm nervous. His eyes sparkle, the flame of his magic dancing across his skin, before he quickly extinguishes it. Still, even without the heat of the flame lighting our faces, I stare up at him, not daring to be the first to look away.

"You're like me," I whisper. I speak low, soft, but he hears my whisper and the desperation in my voice. I've longed for someone like me for what feels like forever, and finally, I found him.

He nods, jaw clenched. He swallows, and his throat bobs. I'm so close, I can see the vein in his neck and the lighter strands of brown in his hair. His crimson irises are swirling with color and life and *power*. Utterly mesmerized, I can't look away.

"Why didn't you come sooner?" I ask.

"I had to find you first."

"But last night… You found me then. Why wait until now?" I ask.

"I needed to wait until you left your nest," Will says.

I frown. "But the others—"

"I have no concern for them."

"They're my family," I say, hurt by his confession.

"Just because they *made* you doesn't mean you're indebted to them. Leave with me." He trails his fingers along my jawline, rubs his thumb gently in the divot of my chin, and angles my head toward his.

Time seems to slow as he waits for my response, but I've fallen mute. I don't want to leave the vampires, but something inside me *needs* Will to stay. I yearn for him in ways I don't desire Jasik. Will can offer me something my sire cannot: answers.

EIGHT

Witches are strange creatures. Blinded by an unspoken camaraderie, they protect each other, even if they aren't part of the same coven, even if they don't understand what's right, what's wrong. Being stubborn and headstrong, I succeeded in that life. Prejudice was instilled at birth, and I asked no questions. I believed everything I was told. It's taken everything I have to break free from the beliefs rooted deep within my soul.

I've liberated myself from all save one—my desire to protect those who cannot protect themselves. When I transitioned, I promised myself I would not hurt a mortal. I would not drink from humans, and I would protect Darkhaven from vampires far more terrifying than anything the witches could conjure.

I thought the moment I consciously chose to forsake my upbringing and choose my vampire allies over those who gave me my life's blood would be earth-shattering.

It wasn't.

It was just another day. The sun rose, the sun set, and now those very witches I actively protected from the fiends they fear are forcing me to choose yet again.

I sense their approach, and from the twitch in Will's eye, he does too. Frozen in time, I listen as they chant, knowing full well how powerful a coven can be.

I blink, and everything changes.

I'm assaulted by a force so powerful, I'm thrown backward. No longer staring into Will's eyes, silently begging him to stay a little longer, I'm watching the world fly by in a blur. I slam against a tree, my head smacking the thick, frozen trunk. Stars dance in my head, and my neck burns at the impact. The thick, slow ooze of blood seeps down the back of my skull, and I fall to a heap at the base of the tree.

The smell of blood—*my blood*—clouds my judgment. It coats the air in its tantalizing fragrance and makes my stomach grumble. I lick my lips and blink away the pain. My vision is blurred, so I wipe at my eyes.

As several figures approach, I ignore the trickling of blood that tickles the back of my neck. It's harder to ignore my splitting headache. My body is shrieking at me, screaming in agony.

I grunt, struggling to stand, and I am forced back down again by the invisible magic. These are air witches. Air might be one of the weaker elements—compared to fire—but it is useful at keeping targets distracted.

The force pinning me down is strong, and I worry it's far stronger than me. I fight against it, pushing to stand. My legs burn, and their magic pushes me down harder.

I sink into the frozen earth. An ache works its way through my muscles, settling deep into my bones. Finally, exhausted and gasping for breath, I relent. No longer fighting, I sit back, resting my head against the tree. The bark is jagged and cold. I wince when it scrapes against my wound.

Four witches stand before me, forming a half circle around me and using their magic to pin me to the tree and the ground. I don't know their faces, but that doesn't matter. My war against my former coven is now theirs to bear. The irony of this pointless feud is the loss of so many innocent lives—which the witches claim to protect.

I glance past them and stare into the distance. More witches emerge from the shadows, and all fight Will. My heart races as he dodges a fireball. Blasts of air like daggers in the wind shred through his torso, and he cries out in agony.

I call to him, and the witches cocooning me lash out. When I'm silent and obedient, they halt their attack, as if they aren't truly interested in me at all. It is clear that their target is Will, and unfortunately for them, he's my only key to the puzzle that is my entire existence.

If they want him dead, they'll have to go through me first.

A one-on-one fight against a witch isn't troubling, but a four-to-one fight is. It will take my full strength and tapping into my questionable magic to evade my captors and aid my newfound ally.

The moment I make the decision to end their lives, I feel… different. It's freeing to abolish that connection to my former life, but more so, it's empowering. With the link severed, I can jump into the abyss.

Unfortunately for them, embracing my dark side is going to cost them their lives.

My magic swirls in me. It's a fire pit of energy, a blazing inferno of power and strength that the witches couldn't even hope to harness.

I ball my hands into fists at my sides, squeezing so hard I'm sure I'll crack bone. My knuckles ache, and I scrape them against the frozen earth. The ice shards covering the land aren't strong enough to break skin, but it dulls the pain. It's a welcome distraction from what's boiling inside.

My magic is sparking to life, igniting within the deepest parts of me. It's desperate to be released. It feels as if it has a mind of its own, and I don't fear its ulterior motives. Instead, I yield to it, knowing this darkness will be the only thing to save us.

I dig my fingernails into my palms. I clench my muscles, my arms twitching, until my elbow aches. My magic is bubbling within, and it's only a matter of time before I burst.

I feel it rising in my chest. It burns in my heart and fills my lungs. It works its way up my throat and into my mouth, forcing its way out.

I scream, and when I do, the buildup of magic escapes through my lips. It blasts outward from my mouth, shooting erratically.

No longer in control, I sit as a bystander as my magic thrusts outward and slams into the four witches entombing me. They are flung backward, soaring through the air as they are hit by a blast of energy far stronger than their combined magic.

The witches scream, relinquishing their hold on their own air magic, and crumble to the ground several yards away. They claw at the ground, fighting to stand, to protect themselves, but it is no use. My magic has already stretched from within me and is creeping toward them like heavy fog on a dark day.

When it reaches my victims, it wraps endlessly around their frail frames, encasing them in a fiery tornado. It takes only seconds for the witches to succumb to my power, and like a staked vampire, their mortal bodies combust into ash, with nothing to remember them by but their cremains in the wind.

With my captors eliminated, I stand. My legs are wobbly,

and I teeter as I move forward. Exhausted from using such powerful magic, I take breaths in quick bursts. In shimmering iridescent waves, my power flows all around me. It stretches outward, never straying too far, always connecting to me in some way. After all, I am its host.

The other witches are surprised by my escape, and some weep for their fallen sisters. I ignore them and trudge forward. My legs are heavy, my arms weak. My stomach burns from hunger. Every second I use this magic, my energy depletes. I'm not sure how long I have before I'm too weak to summon it at all.

Two witches attempt to corner me, blocking me from reaching Will. Angry, I throw out my arms before me. The fire in my heart spills from my palms, lashing forward at my attackers. Morphing from a soft, shimmery iridescent glow, it becomes a violent and blinding orange. It breaks through skin, leaving behind gashes in flesh.

One of the witches cries out when I pass her, but I ignore her fear. Instead, I search for Will. I call to him, seeing him battling his own demons. He's wounded and frightened. The anger in his eyes shoots ice down my spine. I suppose this isn't the best welcome to Darkhaven he could have received.

I trip over brush, my ankle twisting awkwardly as I tumble forward. I yelp, landing in a heap of icy snow. Before I realize what's happening, Will is at my side. He lifts me from the mound, and we both watch as the remaining witches surround us.

Leaning against him, I attempt to cocoon us both within my magic, but I'm growing far too sluggish. I anticipate the other witches will combine their strength, and in my weakened state, I'm not confident I can withstand their fury.

"We need to get out of here!" I shout.

The witches lock hands, forming a half circle before us. Immediately, the elements are bared. The wind whips my hair feverishly around my face. The snowflakes falling become plump and moist, blurring my vision as clusters of ice collect around my eyes. Slowly, Will and I dip into the earth. The frozen ground at our feet turns to mush, and we sink deeper into the mud.

Before we can escape, another witch approaches us, her dark gaze as black as night. Her cheeks are pink, her lips chapped as she shouts an incantation. Her hair whips around violently as her element is intensified by her allies.

She stands before them, a leader before her coven. She's floating, carried by air. Her ankles slack, the tips of her toes pointing directly to the ground as she's lifted by her magic.

With arms outstretched at her sides, she shouts several Latin incantations, and her magic rushes at us. Hardened bullets of beaded air, the wind assaults my magical barrier, tearing it down with little effort.

Other witches stand beside their leader, lending their strength to intensify her magic. With each air shard working its way deeper into my magical shield, I begin to feel the effects of wielding a power far stronger than me.

I slump beside Will, letting him carry my entire weight. My forehead is slick from sweat and snow, my nerves raw. My head aches, and my stomach growls.

"I can't hold on anymore," I whisper, closing my eyes.

The moment my magic dissipates, evaporating into the air and sinking back within my core, Will steps forward. He wraps one arm around my body to hold me upright and lashes forward with the other. A blast of swirling white light tears through his palm and shoots forward.

The surprised witch screams and attempts to protect herself, but it's too late. He mimicked her air blasts and sent his directly to her heart. She falls to the ground, her legs buckling awkwardly beneath her. Her head slams against the frozen ground, and her lifeless eyes stare at me. I loathe the accusations there, so I look away, instead finding comfort in the other witches' disbelief.

They stare at Will as if he too is floating. They expected magic from me, but now they know there is another half-breed. I'm not sure if I should be happy the witches fear us or if I should worry about the target etched into Will's back. I fear he will regret coming to Darkhaven.

I exhale sharply as the witches retreat, choosing to abandon their fallen. Though I'm not surprised by the witches' actions, I feel sorrow for their dead. Why does abandonment come so naturally to them?

"You shouldn't have done that," I whisper.

With my magic now safely tucked inside my soul, I grow stronger. Still weakened by the attack, I push away from Will's embrace and find comfort in the distance I put between us. I'm grateful for his help, but I'm still not sure if I can trust him. I want to believe I can, and after everything he's done, he deserves my trust. But I'm living in a time of war, and trust is not easily given.

"They made my decision for me," Will says. "It was them or us."

I glance at him and notice the darkness in his eyes. I wonder if it's hard for him to kill a witch—since he once was one. Or has time hardened him to the realities of this life as a hybrid creature?

"They'll never forgive you for this," I warn.

"I don't expect their forgiveness."

I consider explaining what it means to have a target on your back in Darkhaven, where there are more witches than humans, but I don't bother. I'm guessing Will has been alive a lot longer than me, and in that time, he's probably made enemies. Still, he risked his life to save mine. That must mean something.

"Thank you," I say softly, sincerely.

"You're too young to be harnessing that much power, Ava," Will warns.

I nod. Holland warned me about this too. If I tap into too much too soon, I risk death.

"I can't control how much comes out," I explain. "It just happens."

"I know, and it will get easier. Control comes with time."

I sigh, letting his words wash over me. The vampires, and even Holland, have said this very same thing to me many times before, but I never believed them. Not until Will, someone who *truly* understands, said them. Knowing I'm living through the hardest parts right now somehow makes this transition easier.

"They'll come back," Will says, scanning the trees around us. "We need to leave."

I nod and stare into the distance. I can still see them running away from us and toward the village. They retreat, and the predator within me wants to follow, to hunt them down one by one.

I look around at the massacre. The snow is stained crimson, and the euphoric scent of blood coats the air.

The witches are dead, and I know I should fear the repercussions of what happened here tonight.

But I don't.

NINE

The silence of the night is unnerving. The forest has never been so calm, so quiet. The loneliness of walking these grounds after every sunset begins to mount.

Is this what my life has become? An endless stream of days sleeping and nights fighting my enemies? A life of watching my back and praying I see the next day? Of watching my step and tracking the shadows? What kind of life is that? Am I even *living*?

I glance over at Will, who's become suspiciously silent himself. I find myself matching his stride as we venture closer to the manor, where my vampire allies await my return. Will they welcome Will as I have? Will they trust him? Should *I* trust him? The constant questions and second-guesses are making my head hurt. In a town full of enemies lurking around every corner, I really should know who to fear, who to trust.

In my heart, I believe Will doesn't intend to hurt me, but I never expected Mamá to forsake me either. I keep wondering who to trust without asking if I can even trust myself. Can I count on my gut, my senses? Or will they betray me too?

"Have you given my request more thought?" Will asks, breaking our silence.

"Hmm?" I say, pretending I have no idea which request he's referring to. It's a lie. I know exactly what he's talking about, and I'm not ready for the truth of my words.

No, I won't leave the vampires, Jasik… I can't. Not because I'm sired to him or because I'm beginning to feel things for him I've never felt for another being before. I feel *safe* with them. It's something I've *never* felt before—not even with the witches. Being with the vampires feels… natural. I always felt out of place with the witches. The hierarchy and expectations were too much to handle. I didn't want to lead my coven, but I am my father's daughter. What I wanted didn't matter. When Abuela stepped down, I was set to take her place. I found comfort in my patrols because the only expectation was to stay alive—and that's one promise I made to myself long ago. I would survive even when others didn't.

With the vampires, I feel connected, loved. We protect each other. They don't rely on me to do everything, and they don't expect me to become something I'm not. And as long as Amicia keeps her weird dark promise ways to herself, I think I can live a long, happy life with them.

"Leave with me," Will says. He stops, and I nearly trip over my feet at the sudden halt.

I turn to face him, crossing my arms over my chest as if I can shield his query with body language alone. I know I can't.

"Will…" I shake my head. *Please don't make me say the words aloud.*

"You don't belong here, Ava. You don't belong with *them*."

"What do you have against vampires?" I ask, arching a brow. Why is Will so adamant that I leave Darkhaven? Doesn't he understand that my entire life is here, in this village? I can't just pick up and leave.

"It's nothing personal," he says. "I just don't know them."

"And I don't know you," I say pointedly. "You're asking a

lot of someone you just met."

"But we're the same. I can help you with things they will never understand."

"Like you said, you don't know them. Give them a chance, Will."

He shakes his head, his decision clear. His eyes are hard, his mouth a sharp line, his brows furrowed. He's disappointed, and I hate that it bothers me.

For what is probably the first time in my life, I'm speechless. I don't know how to answer. I won't leave with Will, but I'm terrified of saying the wrong thing. Because even though I won't leave Darkhaven, I also don't want him to leave either. He's right. He can teach me how to be a hybrid. I need him to stay, and he knows he's holding all the cards.

"Please . . . just—"

"I won't stay here, Ava. I don't belong here."

"I'm not asking you to stay forever. Just stay for now," I say, frowning.

"Is this about the girl? The witch who's missing? Is that why you won't leave?"

Liv. I'm overwhelmed by the fact that I've given her little thought since her disappearance. The guilt smothers me. If the roles were reversed, I doubt she'd care that a newborn hybrid is missing, even if said half-breed is *me*, her former best friend. But I can't just shut off my emotions the way she apparently can.

I've been so busy with my own drama, I'm barely giving my coven's duress a second thought. I imagine they're frantically trying to find her. Right about now, they would resort to invasive magic, attempting to track her whereabouts by any means necessary. But I can't think about that now.

I shake my head and sigh. "No, this isn't about Liv."

"Because if it is, I can help you find her."

My breath catches. "You can?" I don't hide my disbelief.

Will nods. "I'll help you track her. I doubt she's far."

"But... how?" I ask, scratching at my head. My scalp is burning, a tingling sensation washing over me. My senses are warning me of the upcoming sunrise. This would be the time I would start heading back to the manor, especially if I was still a good hike away.

The sun may be rising soon, but there is still plenty of time for answers. I have a couple of hours to work with Will.

"Vampires are hunters, Ava. We're naturally good trackers. Combine that with our magic, and we can be unstoppable if we set our sights on something."

"And you would help me? No questions asked? You would help find a witch?" I ask.

"I would," he says.

His words are like a knife to the heart. The vampires, my *friends*, refused to help her, even when I begged them to reconsider. Will, a *stranger*, is willing to trust that Liv deserves my help based on my word alone. He doesn't know me—or her—but to prove he's an ally and to earn my trust, he's willing to throw caution to the wind and face the witches... again. Considering how our last encounter ended, I'm not so sure they'll want my help now. If Will and I are going to find Liv, we'll have to do it alone—without the help of the coven.

"How can our magic find her?" I ask.

"The elements make up our world, Ava. We harness that magic. It's as simple as that. Well... it won't be *simple*, but you understand what I'm saying."

I nod. "I think so."

"With your connection to Liv and my strength, I think we could easily perform a locater spell to find her."

"But don't you think the witches have done this already?" I ask.

He shrugs. "Maybe they're not strong enough?"

"Maybe..."

I exhale slowly, considering Will's offer. He's willing to help me find Liv, but to do that, I'll have to use my magic again. I have such an emotional relationship with my power. One minute, I love being a hybrid, and the next, I'm cursing this life. Can I be trusted to perform such a powerful spell? What if it goes awry?

"Sometimes this power feels like an extension of myself, but then it seems dark, evil," I admit.

Will is silent for a moment. He frowns, his forehead creasing from his concern.

"I suppose, in a way, it's both. We're unnatural, Ava, and this magic is a physical representation of that. It is all parts of us—the good, the bad, and the evil. It's what you do with that power, how you wield it. That's what determines if it will be used for good or for evil."

"When you put it that way, it's similar to the problems every witch faces," I say, thinking about my past. Sure, I fought to protect the humans of Darkhaven, but I didn't have to. I could have succumbed to the desire to use my magic for personal gain. I had pure, raw energy at my fingertips. I could have used that any way I wished to.

"And every vampire. Any witch or vampire can choose to use his or her power for evil. That doesn't make the source of her magic inherently bad."

I shrug, considering his words. It's not easy being this

powerful and having little discipline. When is it going to be easier? Or will being a hybrid creature always be this hard? Like Will said, we're unnatural. With one foot planted in both worlds, we experience everything. We have the same desires, the same fears, yet we wield the strength to strive for what we crave and abolish what we don't.

"I envy your control," I admit.

Will glances at me and smiles, but it never reaches his eyes. Hidden beneath his happy exterior is a darkness, a longing, an emptiness. Briefly, I see myself in his gaze, and the sight terrifies me.

"Be patient," he says. "You'll get there."

"Time seems to be all we have now," I say, understanding his deeper meaning.

Will nods, his gaze becoming lost in another time, another place. I wonder where he is right now, what he's thinking about. How long has he been a hybrid? How long has he been *alone*? Is that why he yearns for a partner? Is that why he so desperately wants me to join his nomad lifestyle?

"One day, you'll be sitting alone, reflecting on your life and all the things that have unfolded since you became a vampire. You'll stare into that abyss, and the unknown future with a vast amount of time will feel . . . suffocating," Will says.

I'm silent as I consider his words. Will's eyes brighten when he looks at me.

"Don't let it stop you from loving this life. You were given a gift, Ava. You're special. Never forget that."

I hear them in the distance. The distinct smack of feet against the frozen ground grows louder with each passing second. I freeze, worried the witches have returned to avenge their fallen.

Will finally halted his interrogation, and we've been walking back to the manor in silence. Now that we're close, I'm far too exhausted and hungry to properly protect myself, and I can't count on Will to do all the work for me. At least, not *again*.

We glance at each other, and an uncertainty crosses his eyes. He's not sure what to do either. He has no ties to Darkhaven, and I'm guessing if it comes down to it, he will choose his life over another. Unfortunately, that decision doesn't come so easily to me. I have ties here, and they thread together like a noose around my neck.

"We're not far from the manor," I say as I stare into the distance. The woods are dark, and the snowfall is heavy. I squint, seeing nothing but endless flakes. I may not be able to see the manor from this distance, but I know it's there. Somewhere, the Victorian manor is covered in snow, and beneath that roof, my allies await my return.

"Is it normal for witches to hunt so close to your nest?" Will asks, frowning.

I sigh. "Unfortunately, yes. These witches test boundaries and are far too brazen for their mortal coils. Yesterday they showed up unannounced to ask for help. I thought I made myself clear, but today's attack is proof they are still patrolling close to home."

My skin crawls at the thought. How long have they been in the woods? Were they watching me too? Have I not learned my lesson? Distraction leads to death. Plain and simple. I must be the better hunter.

Their footsteps are louder now. They radiate through the ground and up my legs. I grow weaker with each footfall. My throat is dry, my head spinning. What am I supposed to do? Kill more witches? That's not who I am, even if they deserve death. I don't want to be the final straw that breaks, erupting Darkhaven in an endless war. These grounds have seen far too much bloodshed as it is.

"Stay back," Will says, pushing me behind him.

I stumble backward, trying not to fall as I'm forced out of the path of danger. Will steps forward as I voice my disapproval. I don't need him to treat me like a child. I may be weak, but I don't need his protection.

The flash of a fireball erupts within his palm. Will grunts as he flings it forward. The blazing sphere soars through the air, nearly making contact with the flesh of our intruder.

The flash of magic dashes before my eyes too quickly. Pictures of what lies before us dance across my vision, and I choke on my scream. Everything is moving so quickly, and I haven't the time to call out.

The fiery blast was sent prematurely. It was a warning. Will threatened death to those who approach. And he almost incinerated my friends.

Seeing the fire magic's approach, Malik is able to quickly evade the attack. In our many, *many* hours spent in the basement training quarters, he has never shown me the flip maneuver he just used to avoid certain death. He spins through the air, body soaring to new heights, before he lands firmly on the ground once again. The fireball slams into a snow mound several feet away, extinguishing itself and leaving a steaming pool of melted snow in its wake.

"Stop!" I shout, grabbing on to Will's arms and shoving

them down. He spins, releasing himself from my grip, and I nearly lose my footing. I stumble, teetering slightly until I regain my composure. My stomach burns from hunger, and I'm light-headed. I need to feed.

"Ava?" Jasik says. He stares in disbelief. His gaze narrows as he looks at Will.

"Are you okay?" Jeremiah asks. He holds his dagger in his hand, gripped firmly in a white-knuckle grasp. His skin is ashy, his eyes dark. He frowns at Will before looking at me.

"What are you doing here?" I ask.

"It's almost sunrise, and you still hadn't come home. We thought you might be in trouble," Malik says. His face is calm, collected, but his eyes scream with anger. It floods my ears, making concentration almost impossible.

"We didn't realize you had some rendezvous planned with . . . *him*," Hikari says, seething. She crosses her arms over her chest.

They're all rightfully upset with me. I have been gone far too long, and they find me in the dark of night with another vampire—someone they don't recognize and someone I've never mentioned. This certainly does look bad.

"Who are you?" Jasik asks, his gaze on Will.

Will glances at me. He gives me a knowing gaze before answering my sire's question. "I'm Will."

"Are you . . . like Ava?" Malik asks. He eyes Will cautiously, curiously. His gaze drops the length of Will's body, likely assessing the threat level this mystery vampire poses. Unfortunately, Will just might be the greatest opponent Malik has ever faced.

"I am," Will says.

"And how long have you two known each other?" Hikari

asks. She arches a brow, a pointed look in her eyes.

"We've only just met," Will says.

"Seriously?" Hikari says. "You expect us to believe it's entirely coincidental that you've just run into each other tonight? Do you really expect us to believe this wasn't planned?"

"It's true I came looking for her, but she was unaware of my existence until tonight," Will admits. He doesn't mention my dream intrusion or meeting me on the astral plane. I'm grateful, because the last thing I want is for Jasik to believe I truly was keeping secrets.

"Why?" Malik asks, cutting off Hikari.

"Because there aren't many vampires like us," Will says.

"How did you find her?" Jasik asks, frowning. He glances at me, a worried look in his eyes. "How long have you known?"

"There's a lot you don't understand about our powers, and honestly, I don't care to explain them to you," Will says plainly. "I know enough."

Jasik steps forward, and I rush between them. We can't fight about this. Not now. We have only a couple of hours until sunrise, and we need to get home. We don't have time to talk logistics, even though I too am itching to know how Will was able to find me in the astral plane. Are we strong enough to find anyone? Is that how he plans to locate Liv? He mentioned a locater spell, but maybe we do that through the astral plane and that's why the other witches haven't found her yet.

Ignoring my silent plea for peace, Jasik says, "And you expect us to simply trust you?"

"Do what you like," Will says. "I'm here for her."

"Will," I say sharply, and he smirks at me.

I glance at Jasik, and something flashes behind his

crimson irises. I see anger and pain and just a hint of jealousy. It breaks my heart to see him so conflicted simply because of a misunderstanding.

"We need to get home," Malik says. He rests a hand on Jasik's shoulder, and instantly, his brother is soothed. The anger in his eyes is replaced by mistrust, and he turns away from me.

The others begin their retreat, not turning away from Will as they walk backward toward home. I wonder if they'll walk the entire way like this, forever fearing to turn their backs on a possible enemy.

"Ava, let's go," Malik says. It's an order, and I don't particularly care for it.

I hesitate, and I've never heard silence quite this loud. It's earth-shattering enough for the others to break their concentration and look at me. Frozen in time among the icy blue woods, I am forced to choose, but *I can't*. I literally cannot move. My limbs are failing me; my brain is mush. I remain still, silent.

If I leave with Jasik, I risk never seeing Will again.

If I leave with Will, I will surely lose Jasik.

Darting my gaze between my two futures, I stand at a crossroads. I know I cannot stay here, for it is nearly daybreak. I explain this to my legs, but they still do not move. I'm frozen in place, stuck in a pit of darkness and despair. Inside, I beg for a way out, for a way not to choose. But even I know this is no fairy tale. The undead don't get a happily ever after.

Every second that passes, I sink a little deeper into the snow. With each free-falling flake, I'm buried more, and I welcome it. Beneath this white blanket, I can escape the hardship of the world. It embraces me in its cool caress, and even if only for a moment, I pretend life is good.

Everything is perfect.

Until it's not.

"Ava, let's go *home*," Malik says, repeating himself.

I glance at Will, and with my eyes, I beg him to come with, to join us, if only for tonight. I plead with him, silently promising things I have no right to promise. I offer him refuge with my nest, even though I know he will refuse.

Understanding my pleas, he smiles but shakes his head and says, "I don't belong with them."

Silently, I hear his final words—the ones he doesn't dare speak aloud.

And neither do you.

My heart falls from my chest and sinks into the ground. That's where I leave it. It will remain there—cold, lifeless, waiting for some promised future that will never come to pass. Against everything I feel to be true and right, I make a decision to remain in the dark. Forever.

When I turn away to join the others, I feel Will's gaze at my back. It burns through my skin, penetrating deep into my soul. Leaving Will in the lifeless, dark woods feels like a betrayal to everything I am, to everything I could become. He might be the only creature on this planet who completely understands me. He knows my needs, my desires, my faults, and my fears—because he experiences them too. He doesn't judge my emotions or question my motives. He knows me... for me. He knows the hybrid better than even my sire.

The moment the tiny hairs on my body rest, I know he's gone. I glance over my shoulder, knowing he won't be there but hoping to still see him staring as I retreat.

The emptiness of the surrounding woods is like a dagger to my heart.

TEN

There's something about the flutter of snow when it blows in the breeze. Swirling through the air, it coats the earth, hiding evidence of what lies beneath. Hardened by time, what was once soft and yielding is now frozen in place. I kick at the fluff, scraping my boot against the icy, frigid remains of an earlier snowfall.

Straight ahead, the manor towers over me. Passing the wrought-iron gate, I eye it carefully. From the outside, it seems eerily quiet. I assume the other vampires have already made their way to their rooms, awaiting the sunrise.

The footfalls of my fellow hunters echo all around me. The sound radiates through the icy tundra Darkhaven has become and tickles the soles of my feet.

Scanning our surroundings, I see nothing but splashes of frost. It coats the manor. With sharp edges and delicate overhangs, the Victorian architecture stands out in this small, idyllic village. No other house is quite as breathtaking. No other house is home to a nest of vampires either. If I'm forsaken from yet another home, I really will have to leave Darkhaven.

I glance at my sire, who has yet to look me in the eye since I turned my back on Will. Jasik believes I've been dishonest. He thinks I've been orchestrating secret rendezvous with a vampire I don't truly know. This isn't the case, and eventually

I'll be able to explain what really happened in the woods tonight—from meeting Will to fighting the witches. Until then, I must face their wrath.

I glance at the others. They too refuse to look my way. No one is happy with me, and I fear what Amicia will say when she finds out. I thought they'd be happy to discover the existence of another hybrid. Will doesn't just provide answers to far too many unanswered questions—he's also the key to everything I will become. He knows the darkness in me and the magic nestled there. He knows what will happen when it consumes me. He knows what I should fear and what I should protect. Why can't the others see him as an asset?

I eye the second story, easily finding the window to my bedroom, but something else catches my attention. A vampire watches our approach. Her crimson gaze penetrates deep into my soul, as if she already knows about my betrayal. Her hair is long, thick, and black as night. Her skin is pale and luminescent in the moonlight.

When she notices me staring at her, she quickly glances away, pretending to fidget with the drapes. She adjusts the shades, closing them so no light can penetrate the room while she slumbers. In the blink of an eye, she's gone. No longer in view, she retreats inside the manor, where so many others await our return.

A stone path leads me toward the manor's front door. Each slab of rock is slick from the recently fallen snow, but I navigate them with conditioned ease. I consider how long I've been here. It's been long enough to call this place home but short enough to still question my place within the nest. When I first arrived, Amicia warned me that even one mistake will cost me her loyalty. Since then, I have tried to prove myself to her, to the others. I *want* to be here. Leaving Will in the dark must prove that to them.

Slowly, I ascend the steps of the wraparound front porch. When I reach the top step, I glide my fingertips over the frosted head of a gargoyle. I can't even walk inside the house without greeting our protector. His stone head is cold and rough, sending shivers down my arms.

The solid oak door is stained dark. It matches the rest of the wood inside the manor. Large bay windows are to the right of the front door. With stained-glass windows, the moonlight sends a rush of cool gray splashes of light into the parlor. With the room lit, I see the bookshelves, the fireplace aflame, and the tiny table with a half-played game of chess, which now gathers dust.

The front porch wraps around the left side of the manor. It cascades almost completely to the backyard, ending at a comfortable gliding porch swing. I imagine sitting there, enjoying the silence, the darkness, the calm.

I sigh, gripping the handle of the front door, and twist. Just as I suspected, the main level is vacant. Even Amicia has retreated to her room. Silently, I thank the gods for this moment of peace. If I'm going to explain myself, I should speak with Jasik first. One at a time, I will prove my innocence.

Without a farewell, the vampires push past me and ascend the stairs to the second floor. The only vampire who stands beside me is Jasik. I follow them into the adjoined sitting room and watch their retreat. Just as Malik rounds the corner at the first stair landing, he glances over his shoulder. We make eye contact, and in the split second he looks at me, I see his disappointment. He's upset with my actions and fearful of what I might do next. Before I can react, he's gone, rounding the corner and disappearing upstairs. With each stride, his steps grow quieter until I can't hear him at all.

I don't dare look at my sire. Instead, I kick at the floor, scattering dust with my shoe. I crinkle my nose at the sudden intrusion and wait for Jasik to speak.

When the silence becomes too much to bear, I succumb to the pain in my gut that's growing stronger by each passing second. Heading straight for the kitchen, I bypass the dining room and walk through the butler's pantry. I push open the door to the kitchen with far more force than necessary, and it smacks against the wall. I wince as wood makes impact with tile.

The kitchen is as barren as the rest of the house, with no one to invade my thoughts. I thought I wanted to speak with Jasik alone, but his disappointment in me is making it hard to breathe.

Opening the refrigerator, I bypass a mug and tear through the packaging with my teeth. I slurp the cold, thick substance, sucking down every droplet until the suction of plastic is too much to bear. I repeat this process until I've drained several blood bags. I lick away the coating on my teeth, and with a full belly that soothes my nerves, I face Jasik.

My sire is leaning against the kitchen wall directly across from where I stand. With one foot kicked back resting against the floorboards, his arms are crossed, and he's watching me closely. He doesn't speak.

Watching the frustration and anger cross his face breaks my heart. I never meant to upset him by keeping so many secrets.

Unable to stare into his eyes any longer, I close the space between us and slide my arms through his. Loosening his grip, he allows me to wrap myself around his torso, and I rest my head against his chest. Closing my eyes, I pretend today is just another day. We're not at war with the witches, the hunters aren't angry with me, and Liv isn't missing. Briefly, Will doesn't exist, but when I open my eyes again, the reality of my world sinks in, and I pull away from Jasik.

"I'm sorry," I say.

"For what?" Jasik asks, eyes hard. He wants honesty, and I'm prepared to give it to him, even if that means upsetting him further.

I sigh. "Last night, when you came into my room, I was having a nightmare."

He nods. "I suspected you were."

I usher him over to the kitchen table and take a seat. He follows me and rests his arms on the tabletop. The tension in his shoulders is starting to ease, and I just now notice the exhaustion in his eyes. It seems I'm not the only one experiencing sleepless nights.

"Thing is, my nightmare was *real*," I say. "I mean, it wasn't a nightmare at all."

He frowns, thoroughly confused, and waits for me to continue.

"Spirit witches can visit the astral plane. That's where I was when I first met Will," I admit.

Jasik winces at the sound of my new friend's name, but I pretend not to notice. I'm not sure why Jasik dislikes Will, but I assume it's not just mistrust. Jealousy is mixed in there, and I doubt Jasik wants me to know how much power our relationship has over his own emotions.

"How long have you been seeing him?" he asks, voice calm, collected. Inside, I suspect he's at war with his emotions.

He wants me to tell him the truth, even if the truth brings only pain.

"Tonight was the first time we met in person," I say.

Jasik sighs, and he begins to fully relax. He leans back against his chair, clasping his hands together and resting them atop the tabletop. He waits for me to continue.

"You see, dreams are tricky. Sometimes they're prophetic. They warn me of incoming danger. Other times, I'm not dreaming at all. My soul is visiting the astral plane, and everything that's happening is *real*. It's just not happening here, on the physical plane," I say. I smack the wood with my hands, emphasizing what it means to be here physically. These two planes of existence are tricky to navigate and even harder to understand if you're not a spirit witch.

"Okay..." Jasik says, trailing off.

"We don't know anything about my powers now, but even before I transitioned, there still was no guide to understanding my magic. It is up to the spirit witch to dissect the dream. On my own, I had to determine if I was experiencing a vision, if I was visiting the astral plane or just plain dreaming. Unfortunately, this hasn't gotten easier since I became a hybrid."

"It sounds...complicated," Jasik says.

"Complicated is an understatement. For weeks prior to my transition, I felt this dark cloud over Darkhaven. There was this...ominous presence, and now, I understand it was a premonition of sorts. Spirit foresaw my death, and my powers were warning me."

Jasik nods, his eyes urging me to continue.

"But no one believed me. Mamá thought I was too young to foresee such a catastrophic event. She believed I was naïve, and that's the pain of it. My powers were mental. I couldn't *prove* what I saw. I just needed her to trust me. She didn't." I shrug. Every day, the realization of this becomes easier to bear. It doesn't hurt as much, knowing how little my own mother trusted me.

"And how does this affect what's happening now?" Jasik asks.

"Well, last night, after I visited the astral plane and met Will for the first time, I thought I was having a nightmare. I wasn't convinced he was real. After meeting that rogue vampire who said there were more out there... I assumed I was unintentionally influencing my dream."

"And you can do that? Influence your visions?" Jasik asks.

I shake my head. "No, I can't influence a *vision*, but I can influence a dream or a nightmare. It's up to me to figure out if what I'm seeing is real or my imagination."

"And this is why you didn't tell me about the dream last night?"

I nod. "I wasn't sure if it was real, and then everything was happening so quickly. I was training, and Liv was missing, and that whole dark promise with Amicia had me really messed up, and I just couldn't focus and—"

"Wait. What? What dark promise?" Jasik asks, interrupting me.

I suck in a sharp breath and slowly release it. This is it. Either I tell my sire about the oath now or I hide it from him forever. Since I had no idea what I was doing and truly had no intention of forming an alliance with another sire, I pray Jasik will understand. Until now, he's always trusted me. I need to believe in him and our connection.

I look past Jasik. Windows offer glimpses into the backyard, which is dark and frozen. Patches of an icy tundra are illuminated by the moonlight, but the surrounding woods are shaded and gloomy. The forest is lifeless this time of night. The few hours before the moon rests and the sun rises are always eerily quiet. The dead of night outside mirrors the emptiness within the manor, and a cold chill works its way through me.

"The other day, when the witches came here for help, when Amicia sent you and the other hunters out of the manor, she forced me to make a dark promise, a blood oath."

Something flashes behind Jasik's eyes. His query and concern vanish almost instantly. His crimson irises darken, morphing into fiery balls of fury. His gaze hardens, his jaw clenching. His entire body tenses at once, and he sucks in a sharp, staggeringly loud breath. I can hear his teeth grinding as his gaze narrows.

"She *what?*" Jasik seethes. His words are sharp, like daggers directed at my soul. They penetrate deep, and I freeze. I stumble over my words. I don't know what to say, what to think, what to do. I just want to fix this.

I've never seen Jasik so angry, furious with something I've done. Even his hatred for Will was laced with concern and fear, but now, even that's gone. What remains is raw, pure outrage.

"I—I... She made me. I didn't know what it was. I—"

"Did you drink from her?" he asks. He speaks slowly, calmly, and I've never heard so few words hold so much weight.

I shake my head. "No, of course not."

"What did she make you do?" Jasik asks. He rises abruptly and rounds the table. Standing beside me now, he towers over me. I break his gaze, unable to look into his eyes any longer.

"I—um, she cut my palm and then cut hers, and then she made me promise not to look for Liv by myself."

He exhales sharply and shakes his head. Closing his eyes, he squeezes the bridge of his nose. With shaking hands, he mumbles under his breath, but I don't understand him. And I'm almost too scared to ask him to repeat himself.

"Hmm? What?" I ask softly.

"I said, I can't believe she'd do this." He opens his eyes and looks at me. They're void of emotion. Empty pits that spill into an abyss. "To do this to *her* vampires is one thing, but with *you* . . ." He shakes his head and breaks our gaze.

"What do you mean?" I ask.

He turns quickly, shoving his hands through his hair, tousling his already messy style. He slams his fist against the island counter, and the noise radiates through the kitchen walls. I tremble where I sit, watching him, unsure if I should walk over to him or wait for him to respond. When he faces me again, he looks different.

"You are *mine*, Ava. You do not belong to *her*," Jasik says.

Never have I seen him so . . . dominant. He radiates power and strength and a raw animal drive to claim what he sired. Something inside me stirs. Jasik awakens a primal instinct, and it takes everything I have not to touch him, not to push my body against his and let him demand what is *his*.

I've never wanted to be overpowered, but at this moment, I want Jasik more than I've ever wanted anything in my life. I'm shaking, quivering down to my very soul. Jasik watches the effect his words have on me, a sly grin curling the edge of his mouth. I swallow hard and gnaw on my lower lip.

Jasik walks toward me. He strides around the center island, and when he reaches my side, he grins down at me, a mischievous glint in his eyes. My breath catches.

He rests his fingers under my chin and angles my head to

look into his eyes. I stand, resting my palms against his chest. His eyes are a pool of darkness and desire. It steals my breath and races my heart. The room is swirling around us, and I'm suddenly light-headed. I can't break our gaze or move away from him.

Someone clears his throat, and I jolt away from my sire as if I were doing something wrong. I jump back so fast and slam against the chair I was sitting in. My knees buckle, and the back of the chair juts into my kidney as I fall into it. I wince at the pain, but Jasik steadies my fall. His skin is scorching hot against my own flesh, and I back away from him, not expecting the surge of electricity that works its way into my body at his mere presence.

I glance over at our intruder and quickly smile at Malik, who watches our exchange with a curious look. I suppose all the ruckus he overheard made it sound like Jasik and I might be fighting. Instead, he walked in to find an unexpected embrace.

My emotions are erratic around my sire, and I assume the rest of the house can feel it too. We're hot and we're cold, never giving into our feelings but not exactly straying away from them either. It's frustrating and annoying, and I can only tolerate the inner turmoil for so long.

"I thought I'd check in on you both," Malik says. Per his usual conduct, he is emotionless, and for once, I'm grateful. I don't need nor request his input at the moment. I have more important things to worry about than my love life, which is why I fear I really might burst if Jasik and I don't get some much-needed alone time.

"We're fine," Jasik says quietly.

I wonder if he's embarrassed by our exchange. I'm a newborn vampire. My emotions are erratic. He's older, experienced, and supposed to have his crap together. He should be the level-headed one who makes me question my actions. He's not supposed to instigate these kinds of exchanges.

"I can see that," Malik says, voice deadpan.

"We were just talking about..." I trail off, remembering how we left our conversation. The dark promise I made to Amicia is a touchy subject, and I'm not sure I should mention it again.

"She made a blood oath with Amicia," Jasik says. He doesn't bother to hide his annoyance.

Malik nods and eyes me. He doesn't tell Jasik that he already knows about my sacred oath to another sire, but he doesn't lie to his brother either. Instead, he remains quiet, watching the two of us, waiting for our reaction to Jasik's confession. Thankfully, my sire doesn't seem to notice Malik's odd behavior.

"She promised not to look for the missing witch on her own, so no harm done. She promised nothing binding," Jasik says.

I frown and glance at Jasik. What does he mean my words aren't binding? How is this dark promise not something harmful? I thought admitting what I'd done would make me feel better about it, but I'm only left with more questions.

"Will you speak with Amicia about this?" Malik asks.

He eyes his brother carefully. Jasik may be my sire, but Amicia is his. He has remained devoted to her, loyal in her pursuit to protect her other vampires and rid the world of rogues. I was so focused on how this oath is affecting me, I never considered how it might hurt him.

Jasik doesn't respond. His eyes are hard, his body tense. His reaction to Malik's question answers what his lips will not. He will definitely be speaking with Amicia about her role in my life. He doesn't need to admit to that aloud. I just hope he doesn't make things worse. I can't handle yet another feud right now.

"And what about the boy?" Malik says, changing the subject.

"Tonight is the first time they met in person," Jasik says.

"I see," Malik says.

He looks at me, his eyes sharp. He wants me to break, to be honest, but what he doesn't understand is that I am telling the truth. I had no idea Will existed, and I would never betray my nest. I have always been loyal to my friends, my family. And that loyalty came with a price. It cost me my life. I hope the cost isn't quite so extravagant this time.

"I had no idea he was coming here or looking for me," I say. "I don't know him at all. Like you, I thought I was the only hybrid, but we were wrong."

"You say you don't know him, yet you wanted him to come back here, to stay with us," Malik says.

"Do you blame me? If you thought you were the only vampire in existence and then you encountered another, would you not react the same way?" I ask. Doesn't he see how judgmental he's being?

"She wants answers, Malik," Jasik says.

"I understand that, but your duty is to this nest, Ava. You are a hunter. You must protect them."

I nod. "I know, and I wouldn't have asked him to come here if I thought he was dangerous."

"How can you be so sure he's not?" Malik says. "You just admitted you don't even know him."

I shake my head, exhaling sharply. How can I explain this

to him? How can I explain this *feeling*? "I don't expect you to understand."

"Try," he says. "I need to understand, Ava."

I sigh. "I just... I *feel* something when I'm around him. It's like... we're connected or something. I mean, it's not the same as my connection with Jasik. That feels like a true, real connection that actually exists because he sired me. But there is *something* between Will and me. Maybe it's because we're both... different, special. A camaraderie. It's unspoken, but it's there. I truly believe he doesn't want to hurt me."

"Perhaps, but what are his feelings toward these vampires? Does he harbor the same respect for them as you believe he does for you?"

"I—I don't know," I say.

"I think you do," Malik says.

"Enough of this. Ava, do you want to leave with him?" Jasik asks, his voice soft.

"I—" I shake my head. "Why would you ask that?"

"He didn't want to come here, and he doesn't belong in Darkhaven," Jasik says. "Why else would he come here? He wants you to join him, doesn't he?"

I nod and whisper, "He does."

"And do you want to leave with him? Or do you want to stay with us?"

I swallow hard, words escaping me. Suddenly, I'm no longer strong or standing in this kitchen. I'm a child in the arms of my mother. We're in the forest, retreating without Papá. He fights the vampire who ambushed us, and I hear his screams in the distance. Never have I felt so... weak, so alone.

"Don't lie to me, Ava," Jasik says. "I can see the effect he has on you. You hesitated then, when we were in the forest.

And you're hesitating now."

"Do you want to leave with him?" Malik says, emphasizing each word.

"I— No. I don't want to leave, but I don't want him to leave either. He has answers, Jasik. He can help me understand better than anyone else. He knows more than you or Amicia or Holland, and I can't lose him. I can't lose that connection to what I am."

"I know you're scared, but we *can* help you," Jasik says. "Your training sessions were working. You were growing stronger and handling your magic better. Don't give up yet, Ava."

I shake my head and whisper, "Please, don't make me choose."

"Because you would choose him?" Jasik asks, not bothering to hide his pain.

"This isn't about you or him. This is about understanding *what I am*. So if you force me to choose, I will choose *me*."

ELEVEN

The moment Amicia enters the room, the air shifts. The tension tightens like a noose, and I choke. She has a staggering aura regardless of where I am or what I'm doing. It's unsettling, overpowering, and downright disturbing. Sometimes I wonder if she's the oldest vampire alive. Who else could harness such power or inflict such a visceral reaction?

The only thing stronger than my initial fearful reaction to her presence is my anger with what she made me do. It boils in the pit of my gut and is bubbling over. I know it will spill from my lips, and I won't be able to control my fury.

From Jasik's earlier reaction, Amicia's request to form a blood oath with me was unacceptable. She knew what she was doing, what she was asking from me, a vampire sired to another. I was a novice, a newborn hell-bent on pleasing the woman offering me shelter. I trusted her in my weakest moment, and she betrayed that trust. Now I want answers. I want her to apologize for what she did and explain why she would ask that of me.

"What is the meaning of this?" Amicia asks.

Her hair is pulled back into a tight bun. She's wearing black silk pajamas. The pants are too long for her short stature, so they bunch at her heels and slide across the floor as she walks. With arms crossed, she taps her pointer finger against her arm, impatiently awaiting a response. Her gaze is narrowed, and it darts between the three of us.

Jasik steps forward, his anger evident, but before he can ask about Amicia's intentions, his brother steps forward.

"There was a situation while Ava was on patrol," Malik says, breaking the silence and probably saving his brother from being ousted.

Jasik is just as upset as I am, and I want answers just as badly as he does. But we must be smart about this. If cornered, Amicia can outsmart and outmatch us both. Malik is no idiot. He intervened intentionally.

"What happened?" Amicia asks. "Rogues again?"

"Ava met another hybrid," Malik says.

My heart nearly stops at his words. Hearing them aloud when spoken to our leader, the sire of everyone in this nest save for one, is an entirely different experience. Even telling Jasik, my own sire, didn't send such a rush of fear to my heart. I wait for her reaction. Shockingly, Amicia maintains her composure. The only evidence of her surprise is her widened eyes. Her gaze lands on me before she regains her composure.

"You met another?" Amicia asks me. Her voice squeaks as she speaks. Clearly, she too expected me to be the only one in existence. So what does this mean? How does this affect my place in this nest?

I nod, watching her carefully, wondering what she'll ask next. Will she be as upset as the others? Or will she want to meet Will? Will she invite him to stay too?

"Who? Where? Tell me everything," Amicia says.

"His name is Will, and I've only just met him." I don't bother explaining our initial encounter on the astral plane. Spirit is an unusual power that vampires don't understand,

and honestly, I don't care to speak with Amicia any longer than I have to. I'm still upset with her, and I'm already itching to leave. Not only am I annoyed by the blood oath, but I also hate the way she makes me feel inferior to her without even trying. In a lot of ways, she reminds me of Mamá.

"How did he find you?" Amicia asks. That seems to be the question on everyone's mind today. It's a valid concern, but honestly, I don't even care *how* he found me. I just want to know *more* about our powers.

"I'm not sure," I say. "Magic, I guess."

Even as I speak, I know my answer will not please her. She will want more information, but I don't have time to discuss this now. I need to speak with Jasik about Will's offer. If he can help me find Liv, then I don't need the vampires' help. If I leave soon, I can return before sunrise. I glance at the clock. Time is running out.

Amicia frowns, catching my attention. For a moment, she's lost in thought. I'm sure she's asking herself the same questions I've been wondering too. I don't know much about Will, but unlike the other vampires, I want to get to know him. I want to learn more about him and about what we are. What are the limits to our magic? I've already discovered I can touch the cross. What else can I do? Maybe I can drink holy water and eat real food too.

"Where is he now?" Amicia asks.

"I don't know. I asked him to come back with us, but he refused."

"I'm not surprised," Amicia says. "He doesn't know us, Ava. He doesn't know *you*."

"I think he knows he can trust me," I say defensively. I don't want to have this argument again. Not with Jasik or the others or Amicia. I'm done defending my decision to spend more time with Will, the only other hybrid I've met. Heck, he might be the only other one in existence, and that makes him important to me. Why is that so hard to understand?

"How can you be sure *you* can trust *him*?" Amicia asks.

She brings up the same points from earlier, and I groan internally. I can't help my eye roll. This time, I don't have to answer.

"He trusts her enough to ask her to leave with him," Malik says, emotionless. It's moments like this I want so desperately to read his mind.

This time, Amicia does not hide her shock. She gasps, her gaze darting between Jasik and me. Still seething, Jasik hasn't spoken to her or met her eyes. He's fuming, breaking at the seams, trying desperately to maintain his composure. Amicia either doesn't notice or doesn't care that he's waging an internal war over what she's done.

"He asked you to leave Darkhaven?" Amicia asks.

"He did," I say firmly.

"And do you plan to go away with him?" Amicia asks. I appreciate her candor. I don't have time for games.

I'm silent as I think about everything that's happened in my life until this point. I owe the vampires so much. Without them, I would have died a long time ago. But even though they've shown me the true meaning of family and support, they've also done things I can't condone.

They forced me to choose between my life with them and saving an innocent from my past. I vowed loyalty to the nest, yet Amicia didn't believe that I would stand by my word. After essentially brainwashing me into doing her bidding, I'm not sure I can trust her anymore.

"I haven't decided," I say, narrowing my gaze. I'm not so sure Amicia will appreciate my honesty as much as I appreciated hers just a second ago.

"And why is that?" Amicia asks, frowning. She actually has the audacity to look hurt—offended, even.

"Because I want to live with vampires I trust," I say pointedly.

"You don't trust us?" Amicia asks. Either she's an excellent actress or she is truly, thoroughly confused by my confession.

"I don't trust *you*," I admit.

Amicia blinks, considering my words. Several seconds pass, and she simply stares at me. I refuse to be the first to break the silence. If this is a test of power, I will win.

"Why don't you trust me, Ava?"

"Are you kidding? Are you seriously playing the victim here?"

Amicia scoffs, but before she can play the martyr, Jasik steps in, saving me from completely losing my mind.

"You forced her to make a blood oath with you, Amicia," he says. "That is a ritual saved only for sires, and you know it. By casting your presence in her life in that way, you've essentially demoted me. If anyone had done this to one of your vampires, you would have killed them."

"Jasik, listen to me. It's not—"

"Stop. Nothing you say can justify what you did. Oaths are binding, Amicia. She is forever bound to you, to this request. There is no breaking it. Her blood is tainted by yours."

Finally understanding why I've felt so... *off* since the oath, I swallow the knot in my throat. I have felt like a foreign essence has plagued my body, and I've wanted nothing more than to shake it free. Amicia is inside me now. Her blood is mixed with my blood, and it will remain there forevermore.

"Why would you do that?" I ask, my voice soft. "Why did you force me to make that blood oath? You knew it was wrong. You knew what you were doing."

I cross my arms over my chest, holding myself. Every second I wait for Amicia to respond, I grow more upset. I'm not just angry with her. I'm . . . hurt. She was well aware that I just left a controlling coven, and she thought it would be a good idea to take even more of my freedom from me?

Scratching at my skin, I feel dirty. I feel her everywhere. Her essence surrounds me, smothering me. I feel like I can't breathe, can't think. I want to get her blood out of my system, but I know I will never be free of her. Jasik's explanation of a blood oath's consequences has made that clear. I have eternity on this planet, and I will spend it with her inside my head.

Amicia frowns, her eyes sad. But is she upset because she's been outed? Jasik knows what she did, and she'll have to answer for it.

The two sires exchange odd glances. Their angry glares are bone-chilling as both wait for the other to speak first. Amicia is the first to budge.

"I didn't have you make the oath as some form of betrayal to your sire," Amicia says when she looks at me. "I wasn't trying to control you. I did it to protect you."

I scoff. "Excuse me? How is forcing me to do this protective? Ever since I took the oath, I've felt . . . different. *Dirty.* I hate myself for doing this with *you.*"

Amicia sighs. "I understand your frustration, but in time, you'll understand. You're new to this life. You think it's hard now, but it is only going to get worse."

Suddenly overcome with anger, I shout, not caring about

containing my rage or being respectful toward my elder. "Stop! Stop acting like I'm some child you must protect. You don't need to shield me from this world. And while you're at it, stop making decisions about *my* life without consulting *me*!"

"Ava, calm down," Amicia says. It is not a request, but I'm too far gone to care.

"No!" I yell.

"I made you take the oath because I know this transition has been difficult for you. Most vampires don't reside so close to their former lives. I wanted to make forsaking the witches easier. I promise, that was my only intention. I don't wish to control you."

"You don't get to decide these things, Amicia. You're not my sire, and you're not *me*. *I* can make my own decisions about how I live my life and the relationships I keep. I don't need you to make my transition easier, and I certainly don't want you to make me some emotionless zombie. I'm tired of being treated like a child!"

"Then stop acting like one," Malik says firmly.

"Excuse me?" I say, seething. I'm starting to understand why he has such trouble expressing his emotions. Maybe Amicia did her voodoo on him too.

"If you want to be treated like an adult, stop acting like a child. It's as simple as that, Ava. You're rash, emotional, and have no respect for authority. While I don't agree with what Amicia did, I understand it," Malik says. He turns to his brother and says, "And you should too."

"What she did was *wrong*," I say.

"Yes, it was. Amicia should have consulted your sire. But Jasik hasn't been able to control you either, so Amicia stepped in."

"*Control me?*" Why does everyone want to *control* me?

"Ava, these witches have given you every chance to walk away," Malik says. "They cast you out and betray you just about every time you rush over to save them. Your ties to them are rooted so deeply, you can't even see how blinded you are by your devotion to them."

"I know you feel I'm trying to control you by performing the blood oath, but really, I was trying to free you from the hold they have on you," Amicia says. "I knew my decision not to help your missing friend wouldn't sit well, so I tried to make it easier for you. I promise, I had no ulterior motives."

"I don't believe you," I say.

"You don't have to," Amicia says, "though it is the truth."

"What Amicia did was wrong—and will *never* happen again—but I do believe her," Jasik says. "You didn't drink from each other, and your promise to her wasn't anything life-changing."

"Seriously? I'm not sure Liv would agree with that," I say. I can't believe Jasik is siding with the very person he was so angry with only moments ago. How does she have this effect on everyone in her life? Is it simply their sire bond, or does she have some magical powers I have yet to learn myself?

"You said you promised not to search for the witch yourself. To me, that does sound like she was trying to protect you," Jasik says. "I know you feel you can trust these witches, but something doesn't feel right about this. The rogue vampires literally just threatened the same thing. How can you trust this isn't yet another trap?"

I shake my head, frustrated. I know he's right. It might be a trap, but I didn't want to risk Liv's life. That's why I asked for their help. And if I am truly tied to them as severely as they say, this would be a good opportunity to sever the ties that bind us. Separating myself from the coven shouldn't mean someone's death.

"Will said he can help me find her," I say softly.

The room falls silent. The vampires exchange sideways glances, not even bothering to hide them. I wait for someone to speak, hoping they will see the error of their ways and offer me the help I—and Liv—so rightfully deserve.

"And you believe him?" Amicia asks.

"I do. I think he wants to prove to me that he's an ally, and what better way to do that than by helping me when my own nestmates refuse to?"

I know my comment is pointed and harsh and a bit childish, but I don't care. I think about my promise to Amicia and Jasik's explanation of what the oath means. I have to abide by it. It's unbreakable, but if she truly meant no harm, then she was just trying to protect me. If she truly believes the witches are a threat, then she wouldn't want me to go alone. She doesn't trust them, yet she believes I still harbor a familial bond. So she would expect me to break my promise to her.

Ever since Liv went missing, I haven't thought much about rescuing her. In fact, the only time I considered looking for her was when I discussed her disappearance with Will.

"That's the secret, isn't it?" I say, pretending the vampires were following my train of thought.

"Excuse me?" Amicia says, her confusion evident.

"The oath cannot be broken, but you only made me promise not to look for Liv *on my own*. I promised not to search for her *by myself*. You never made me promise not to look for her *with someone else*."

"Ava," Amicia says, her tone a clear warning. I shouldn't

be testing her like this, I know that, but she should have been clearer when we made our oath. It's almost as if she intentionally provided me with a loophole just to see what I'd do. Sadly, I am going to fail this test.

"This is my way out," I say. "If I search for her *with someone*, I'm not breaking your oath."

"Do you really believe you can trust him?" Amicia asks.

"I do."

"I certainly hope you can, Ava, because you're risking your life if you can't," Amicia says.

Realizing that the vampires and I will never agree on this, I sigh and glance at Jasik. His wounded heart is betrayed by his longing eyes. He doesn't want me to go, to leave with Will, but I don't think he'll ask me to stay. He understands my desire for freedom and for answers. I can achieve both with Will.

"I don't have a lot of time," I say, glancing out the window. Already, the sky is brightening. If Will and I are going to cast a locater spell, we'll need to do so soon. We can't risk being too far from shelter when the sun rises.

With my head down, I walk past the others, not daring to look anyone in the eye as I retreat. I push open the door to the butler's pantry but stop short of leaving the room when Jasik calls to me. The pain in his voice is unbearable. It's filled with so much sorrow, I'm forced to look at him. As my sire tries to rush to my side, Amicia stops him. She grabs on to his arm, lightly holding him back. He doesn't fight against her.

"Ava must make this decision for herself. She can stay with us or leave with him. Either way, the decision must be hers."

And with one final, painful glance, I leave.

TWELVE

In the distance, I distinctly hear the sound of Jasik's voice. He calls to me, a plea to return. I ignore him.

I'm already running. I exit the manor, slamming the front door behind me as I leap off the porch. I land at the foot of the steps in a heap and then dash through the yard and exit through the main gate. The Victorian manor looms behind me, and I give it one final glance before the woods envelop me.

The wind is fluttering through my hair, tousling what has already become messy from an eventful day. The falling snow coats my skin, and I push hair from my eyes, tucking it behind my ears.

I don't know where I'm going, but I had to escape the manor. Frustrated by Amicia's actions and annoyed with her words, I can't spend another second in her house without doing something I would certainly regret later. Tonight, I need space.

If the others are right and I am blinded by my ties to my former life, then I need to sever them for good. I'm tired of everyone in this town having power over me and my life. Jasik is my sire, Amicia is my leader, and the witches are my life's blood. They all influence my decisions so much, I don't even remember who I am anymore.

But no more.

Tonight, I will take back control. I just need to find Will first.

I return to the last place I saw him and attempt to track him courtesy of winter. I crouch down, scanning the land, but the new-fallen snow has already coated the ground, filling the craters of his footprints.

I curse inwardly and kick at what should have been easy tracking. When I stand, I spin in circles, considering Will's options. We left him earlier to fend for himself, knowing it won't be dark for long. Where would a new-to-town hybrid go? Where could he stay when the sun rises? Or has he already left Darkhaven for good? I fear I'm too late.

Just as I consider shouting his name for the whole village to hear, something rustles in the distance. The sound of brush snapping under weight echoes in my mind. I catch a flash of a figure standing behind a tree, and I cross my fingers that it's him. Finding Liv without Will's help will prove problematic, thanks to the oath I made.

Charging steadfast into the unknown, I run toward the creature, silently hoping I'm not running toward some wicked ambush. I don't have time to fight witches or rogues. I barely have time to perform a locater spell with Will before the sun rises.

By the time I reach the base of a thick pine tree and circle it twice, I realize no one is there. Save for mine, there are no footprints in the snow either. Did I imagine what I saw? Am I so desperate to find Will that I'm now hallucinating help?

I scratch at my scalp, considering my options. Groaning, I begin walking farther into the woods. I'm venturing closer to town and farther from the manor, and I still have no clue where I'm going or what I'll do when the sun rises. Lost in my thoughts, I don't notice the onlooker.

"Couldn't stay away, could you?" someone says.

Heart pounding, I spin to see Will. He leans against a tree, smiling. Relief washes over me, and I waste no time.

"You said you would help me find Liv," I say as I close the distance between us.

He nods. "I did."

His jacket is caked in white, and his hair is damp. I wonder if he waited for me to return to him. Perhaps he knows me better than I even know myself. He must have assumed my curiosity would get the best of me, because he didn't leave when I chose the others over him.

"Does that offer still stand?" I ask.

"It does." He runs a hand through his hair, and it snags in his locks. He brushes strands from his eyes as he watches me closely.

"No strings attached?" I confirm.

He chuckles and throws his arms up in defeat. "I just want to help. That's all. I'm expecting nothing in return."

Satisfied with his answer, I say, "Then tell me what I need to do."

We sit cross-legged in the snow. With my hand, I draw a half circle, connecting the two ends to the opposite side Will has drawn. Together, we sit inside of a fully formed circle—our own version of a perfect ritual space.

Of course, we're missing key items, like candles or relics to represent the elements. We aren't surrounded by a coven of witches, and we don't have a grimoire that harnesses the ancient spells. If we want to find Liv, we must do this by memory, trust, and faith alone.

Even without these things, the familiar pull of magic is already tugging within me. Will's eyes burn brightly as he stares at me, smiling, and I wonder if he misses this. How long has it been since he performed a ritual? How long has he been alone?

I scan our surroundings. This ritual will leave us both vulnerable, but thankfully, the woods are barren. The cold and snow have kept away most animals, and it's too late in the night for passersby. I fear the witches will return, but I pray their earlier loss will force them indoors until the morning.

I think about the last time I completed a locater spell. It's been years. I'm not sure I remember the incantation. If we turned to the coven for help, they would be surrounding us now. They would be chanting in Latin and casting a spell to strengthen our power. Their arms would be cast out beside them, their heads tilted back so they stare at the moon. There would be candles to represent the elements, and they would be harnessing the power of the night.

Will and I have none of these things now. We have no coven to turn to, no spells to rely on. The strength that will save Liv must come from within us. If we—two hybrids—haven't the magic to locate her, no one does. Even so, I can't help but wonder if we're fools for trying such a complicated spell without assistance. What if things go awry? Can I trust Will to bring me back from the edge?

"Are you ready?" Will asks.

His crimson gaze is piercing, and I feel my pulse rising. Practicing magic with someone is an intimate experience. I'm not sure I'm ready to rely on Will, a *stranger*, in such ways.

"I'm not sure what to do," I admit.

"We're going to link and share our power. With my strength and your connection to the witch, I think we can locate her as long as she hasn't gone too far from Darkhaven."

I swallow hard. "And how do we ... link?"

"It's a form of bloodletting," Will says. "Our magic courses through our veins. This is why vampire blood can heal a mortal."

Understanding what's expected of me, I nod, but my nerves never settle. I want to find Liv, but I'm not sure I want to expose myself to Will in this way. Bloodletting is a tricky practice, and it'll be even harder as a half-vampire hybrid. It will take a great deal of magic and strength to do this successfully.

Will smiles, calming my inner turmoil. "Don't worry. I'll do most of the work. You just follow my lead."

I nod and watch as he bites into his wrist, fangs tearing through flesh. My stomach churns as the smell of his blood coats the air. It's thick and nauseating but strangely seductive. I lick my lips, staring at his wound. Blood seeps down his arm, staining the white snow between us in crimson.

"Ava," Will says, breaking my concentration. He ushers me to do the same.

I freeze and think about how Amicia made me commit a far too similar act. Her blood oath ritual ripped away my freedom. No longer able to act on my own, I succumbed to her will and made promises I wasn't prepared to make.

I know Will has no intention of controlling me, but still, the initial fear remains. Bloodletting makes no promises, and though it's a vulnerable practice, it's not the same as a blood oath. If this is the only way to find Liv without asking the witches for help, then I need to let down my guard, walk to the edge, and leap. I must trust Will, or our locater spell will never find her.

I exhale slowly, loudly, but it's unsuccessful at easing my nerves. I bring my wrist to my lips, hesitating ever so slightly. My throat tightens, but I don't stop. The moment my fangs pierce my skin, I taste my own blood. It's sweet and thick and fills my mouth. I slurp it down before pulling away from my wound.

Eyes wide, I stare at my bloody wrist. I tore into my own flesh with every intention of saving the life of someone who wants nothing to do with me. How has it come to this? Why do I keep feeling this innate desire to help the witches, to protect my blood relatives? Amicia was right; being so close to Darkhaven clouds my judgment. Maybe distance is all I need to see things clearly. When this is over, I might really leave with Will and never look back.

"Quickly. Before our magic can heal us," Will says as he slaps his wound to mine.

Wrist to wrist, I grab on to his arm. He does the same. Where our bodies connect, his blood enters my wound, coursing through my veins. Streams of crimson swirling together, I can't sense where his essence ends and mine begins.

Closing my eyes, I sway back and forth, relishing in the feeling of Will's power. It seeps into me, filling my body with raw, pure, untapped energy.

Will is strong—too strong. His strength is similar to Amicia's power, and the thought makes me shudder. Underneath Will's friendly gaze, a dangerous, powerful predator lurks. It reminds me of the foreign presence I acknowledge within my own soul. Something about being a hybrid makes me feel like the magic inside me isn't truly mine, like it knows it's unnatural and shouldn't exist and it has intentions of its own.

The air tingles around us as our blood magic takes control of my mind. It separates me from the physical world, and I welcome its embrace. I no longer feel the cool, brisk air dancing across my skin. The cold snow beneath me vanishes into a pool of warmth. The trees surrounding us are gone. I don't even feel Will's gaze or sense the animals that slumber in the woods.

The manor is gone. The witches are gone. Darkhaven is gone.

There is only Will and his blood inside my veins.

A wave of magic assaults me, and I nearly jolt upright from where I sit. Breathless, I struggle to maintain my hold. He digs his fingers into my flesh, and the pain grounds me.

I want to go back to that place where nothing exists. There was no pain, no pleasure—just eternal nothingness. I wasn't a disappointment, my friend wasn't missing, and I could just be still.

But I know I will find no answers in that place. I sway from side to side as I fight the urge to float away again. My aura, my mind, my entire essence wants to leave this place, this physical plane. But I need to focus. I need to stay here. I have to find Liv.

I open my eyes. With a heaving chest and glossy eyes, Will stares at me. I think he's speaking to me, mumbling words I can't understand. His voice is barely a whisper, and it pains me to focus on what he says, but I do it anyway.

By the time I recognize the Latin incantation, the air is already hot around us. The elements are strengthening as they prepare to locate Liv. When I look into Will's eyes, our surroundings begin to fade away, and our magic regains the control it needs to lead me to *her.*

The world becomes dark, with nothing but Will's piercing crimson gaze rooting me.

Once again, there is only me and Will and the unfamiliar feeling of his essence coursing through my veins.

This time, I don't float away. I stay rooted in the present, on the physical plane, and I clear my mind. I focus on our intention, understanding that Will and I can only hold on to this magic for so long.

My skin is slick, and I ignore the overwhelming urge to reach up and wipe away the sweat that dribbles down my temple. It tickles my skin, and I shake as I shiver.

"Use our magic to locate her," Will says. He whispers when he speaks.

Silently, I call to spirit, using Will's power and my memory to focus on Liv. I remember all the times we shared. I picture her, seeing her as clearly as I see Will before me now. I imagine she's beside me, leading me to her body on this physical plane.

I see her dark hair, her brown eyes, her pale skin. She smiles at me, and it feels like it used to. We're friends again, and I'm just a witch. We laugh and keep secrets. We have our whole lives ahead of us. I'm not dead—and neither is she.

The wind around us grows stronger, the air heating as we connect with Liv. I close my eyes, desperately trying to maintain my control over our combined magic.

"Will . . . I feel her," I whisper.

I sway again, fighting the urge to topple over. Will reaches out, guiding a hand to steady me.

I see flashes of images—all things Liv must have seen. I don't know what's real and what's her imagination. Can I use these pictures to piece together where she is now? I try to, but my mind begins to wander as I tire. Exhaustion is sneaking up quickly, and soon, I'll be too weak to connect at all.

"Stay focused," Will warns.

I nod, my head heavy. I slump over, resting against Will. He wraps his arms around me, and I lean against his chest. His pulse is pounding against my ear. I can't hear anything but his breath and the steady, strong beat of his heart. If I don't pull away from him, I'm certain I'll lose my connection to Liv.

Will must understand because he pushes away, setting me upright. With slick wrists, I nearly break our connection when we move. I dig my fingers into his flesh, desperately trying to grip his arm. Will does the same, and I wince. Our bleeding wrists must stay bound together. The wound tingles as my vampire blood attempts to heal it, but this ritual is meant to maintain this vulnerability. Until we separate, we will continue to bleed into each other.

With both hands, we hold on to each other's wrist. Each second I harness this magic, I feel my energy draining. I'm weakening. My body was never meant to harness the magic of *two* hybrids. With heavy eyes and a sleepy gaze, Will doesn't seem to be handling the power any better than I am. He continues to whisper the incantation, only breaking when he speaks to me.

"Tell me what you see," Will whispers. He sounds pained, and I fight to keep my eyes open so I can look at him.

"I see ... trees. A lot of trees. It's ... remote, very rural. Very cold."

I shiver as if what I envision can actually affect me here, now. I know it cannot—and not because the undead don't experience things like the cold the way the living does. I know what I see is through Liv's eyes. She may be experiencing pain, but it will not transfer to me. I just need to see enough to be able to locate her.

I focus intently on the task at hand, becoming breathless from my exertion. My arm aches, and my stomach grumbles. I'm growing weaker by the minute. I need to see something worthwhile soon, or I'll never find her.

"What else?" Will asks softly.

"She feels close," I say.

"Good," Will says. "Maybe she's still in Darkhaven."

I squeeze my eyes closed as tightly as I can, trying to see through Liv's eyes. I fear what I might witness. She's alive, but is she still mortal? Is she rogue? What will be expected of me if she's a vampire? Will I have to hunt her too?

"I see…" I squeeze Will's hands so tight, my nails puncture skin. He sucks in a sharp breath, and the sound of hissing air pierces my ears. I shiver but don't ask if he's okay.

"Keep going," Will says. "Try harder."

Sweat beads down my forehead and pools in the crevice of my eyes. It stings, and I shake my head to whisk it away.

"Focus, Ava," Will warns. "We haven't much time."

"I see…"

I open my eyes, sucking in a sharp breath. I pull away from Will, yanking my arms free to break our connection. I don't want to see Liv anymore. I don't want to be inside her head or experience what she sees. Will is so surprised by my abrupt disconnect, he releases me with little fight.

I stare at my fellow hybrid, unable to speak. I know my shock is evident on my face, because Will frowns at me. He opens his mouth to speak before quickly snapping it shut again. He's not sure if he should ask, and I'm not sure I want to admit what I saw.

Because what I witnessed changes everything.

"The locater spell worked," I say. "The ritual worked. I connected with Liv and saw through her eyes. I watched her life unfolding as if I were her. But I can't believe what I saw."

"What did you see?" Will asks.

"It can't be true," I whisper, shaking my head.

"What is it? What's wrong?" Will asks, confused.

My wrist tingles, and I glance down at it. My flesh is healing, removing any evidence of our spell. It's as if it never happened. And internally, I wish it hadn't. I wish I'd never cast the spell. I wish I'd never seen what I saw, and I wish I'd never risked my life to save hers.

"What did you see?" Will asks. He swallows, and I stare at his throat. I'm hungry, but the desire to feed is masked by something else. Another emotion rages within me, and it's all I can feel. Never in my life have I felt so betrayed, so furious, so...malicious.

"Ava, tell me!" Will shouts.

"I found her," I say quietly, still unbelieving of what I saw.

"And?" Will asks.

"She's with Mamá."

I'm stomping through the snow, uncaring of how much noise I'm making. Dead brush crunches beneath my feet. Twigs snap, the sound like a whip in my mind. The witches will surely hear my approach, but I don't care. I want answers.

"Ava, think about what you're doing," Will says.

He struggles to keep up with me. I'm familiar with this frozen tundra, but he's not. He trips over fallen branches and crashes into tree banks. He's been trying to calm me down since I broke our circle and began rushing over here. But I can't be tamed.

"I want answers, Will."

"I know, and I do too, but think about this," Will warns. "Think about the timing of this. We just battled another coven, and we're outnumbered. We're weak from the spell."

But I don't care about any of that. I just need to see them. I need to know what happened, why they lied—if Liv was ever missing to begin with. Questions circulate in my mind, and it's all I can think about right now. I don't fear for my safety; I fear for theirs.

"I need to know *why*," I say, repeating myself.

Why would Mamá lie to me? Why would she make me think Liv was taken? She knows Liv was important to me. Was this just some cruel game? Did she think it was funny? Was she testing my loyalties? Was it Liv's idea, or was she an innocent bystander in the witches' messed-up games? I have more questions than answers, and that just frustrates me more.

"Maybe they already found her, and that's why she is with them," Will suggests.

"She didn't seem like she was just saved from her abductors," I say. I smack a low-hanging tree branch as I pass it. A flurry of snow cascades around us, falling to the ground. "In fact, she seemed just fine. Now tell me, Will, if you were just held captive for two full days, would you act like nothing happened? I think not."

"Ava, this is suicide!" Will says, his voice frantic.

"Then wait here," I say. "I'll only be a minute."

Straight ahead, I see Mamá's house. The forest brushes up against her backyard. The only thing separating the two worlds—the forest and her home in Darkhaven—is a short, wooden fence.

I make my way toward the gate and stare at the house I used to find so homey. I liked that Mamá never painted the wooden planks Papá used to build our home. I thought it was sweet, like she was secretly always waiting for him to return to us. It makes me sick to think of the woman he would have come home to. She's nothing like the person he fell in love with.

I peer into the windows, squinting to see shadows inside the rooms. It's too dark inside to see anything clearly. The house looks empty, but I know she's inside, waiting for me. If this was just a test or some sick, twisted game, then she expected me to figure it out eventually. She knows me well enough to trust I would come here for answers.

I open the gate, the creak from weather-worn hardware announcing my presence, and step past the threshold and into her backyard. Will is beside me, but he scans the surrounding woods. He's certain more witches are coming for us, and he might be right. But I can't think about that now.

"*Hola, hija,*" Mamá says.

She steps out of the shadows, where she was waiting, hiding.

"Mamá," I say in response.

"*Sabía que vendrías,*" she says, confirming my earlier thoughts. She was expecting me to return home.

"And what did you plan to say to me when I came back?" I ask. I narrow my gaze at her, hoping my anger is evident.

"Liv was not missing, *mija,*" Mamá says. "She was never in danger."

"You lied to me. But why?" I ask, shocked my coven would stoop so low. "What was the point? Was this all just a game to you?" Faking the disappearance of one of their own was pathetic. They should be above such trivial, childish pursuits.

"*Esto no es un juego*," she says. "After you came to our aid so naturally when the vampires attacked, I knew you would come again. You just needed motivation."

"What do you mean 'this is not a game'? What's going on?" My skin is prickling, warning me of incoming danger.

I glance at Will, who's shaking from nerves or hunger or both. He must feel it too. Something is... off, not right. He stares into the distance, noticing what I was too distracted to see.

We are surrounded. While I was confronting Mamá, the other witches encircled us. Standing in their crosshairs, I have no choice but to wait for their attack. I'll admit, I might not have been on friendly terms with my coven, but they're the last witches I expected to actually hunt me down.

"I had to lie, *mija*," Mamá admits. "It was the only way to get you here."

"And now what? What happens now?" I ask, desperately trying to sound stronger than I am. I'm terrified, and I don't want the witches to sense it.

Are you going to actually kill me, Mamá? Your own daughter?

"Now you come home," she says.

THIRTEEN

I wish I could say I never expected my demise to be at the hands of my own mother, but even I know that to be a lie. Even so, that doesn't make me stop wondering *how* Mamá could betray me like this. From the beginning, she's hated what I've become, but is her animosity, her bitterness toward my new life, really enough to make her feel death is my only way back to salvation?

Time slows as the witches draw nearer. It's almost as if they move in slow motion. I know they're not. It's all in my head, and briefly, I pretend *everything* is in my head. I'm not standing in Mamá's backyard. I'm not facing the witches in what will surely end in a battle. I'm not risking death or fighting those I once loved. I'm in bed at the manor, and everything is okay.

Until it's not anymore.

Frowning, I scan the crowd. There are so many faces I don't recognize. I'm not surprised Mamá asked the other covens to aid her in this ridiculous, spiteful pursuit, but I am shocked so many side with her.

They dive into a world of unknowns, not caring to understand the truth or accept the half-blood creatures Will and I claim to be. They will not have promises of peace and prosperity, and because of this, we will never escape war and bloodshed. I understand that now. I understand that it is either them or me.

When I look at Mamá and stare into her eyes, I do not see sorrow. There is no regret, no anguish. She does not mourn her daughter. She looks at me with disgust, with shame. Am I really so far gone in her eyes? She mourns who I was without considering that which we've gained.

My throat tightens as the witches begin their chants. I inhale sharply, holding my breath as I consider our options. Everything in my life results in death and destruction, yet I can never get used to fighting to the death like we're gladiators.

Will is beside me. He grabs on to my hand, sliding his fingers to thread them between mine. I stand as a united front with a stranger. He does not know me, but he risked his life to save another. I search for her, wondering if she knows the pain she's caused.

I see Liv. She stands beside Mamá, a formidable force with a fireball bouncing between her two hands. It seems I'm not the only one who's been training. She smiles at me, but it does not reach her eyes. Even so, they tell me everything her lips do not. She helped Mamá plan this attack. Together, they worked to kill me.

The weight of Will's hand against mine is almost too much to bear. If only I'd listened to the vampires, if only I'd believed the witches were up to no good, we wouldn't be here. We wouldn't be close to death, and Will would live to see another day. I refuse to be responsible for his end. He's shown me more support in the past day than my coven did my entire life. He deserves my protection; they do not.

"Ava," Will says.

His voice is cold, his tone hard. His gaze is sharply attuned to what's happening around us. I should be as focused as he is, but I can't shake the feeling that confrontation will only make things worse. We will quarrel our way to freedom, but in the meantime, the witches have a plan, and it's nearly sunrise.

Mamá has outsmarted us. From the beginning, she anticipated my reactions. She knew the vampires would not assist her, and she knew I was too stubborn a creature to let Liv die. She was smart enough to foresee my leaving yet another home in favor of what I believed was morally right.

My skin prickles, a clear warning that I cannot rattle. Every day, my skin tingles as the moon sets and the sun rises, but usually I'm safely inside the manor, and often I'm tucked beneath the covers of my bed. I envision it now—cold, empty. I wonder if I'll ever glide beneath those sheets again.

"We need to act quickly," Will hisses.

His pulse is racing, his skin burning. I'm sure if I look into his eyes, I'll see his magic bubbling within them, pools of the raging elements at war with what the witches are executing—*us.*

He's angry, afraid, and forcing me to choose. Our enemies have made it clear. If we want to survive, they will have to die. We can escape their fury tonight, but that means sacrificing anyone who gets in our way, including Mamá or Liv or the countless others whose faces I *do* recognize.

My former coven members look at me with disdain. It feels like a lifetime ago when I would have gladly sacrificed my life to save any one of them. How much can I withstand? How many betrayals do I need to experience before I relinquish control over that selfless girl?

Blinded by devotion to the only blood I've known and terrified by the idea of an eternity without them, I willingly allowed the witches to abuse me. But the cycle ends here. As much as I want to forgive Mamá and love her, I can't. She won't let me.

I squeeze Will's hand three times to let him know I'm ready for an all-out brawl. I'm prepared to fight my way through bloodshed and teardrops if that means we see another nightfall. I wish it didn't have to end this way, but they've given me no other options.

If they want a war, the vampires will give them one.

I exhale slowly and release Will's hand. We separate, him skating to the left, attacking the many witches attempting to control him with their magic, and me rushing to the right, toward Mamá and Liv and far too many familiar faces.

Everything moves too quickly. I don't think about what I'm doing, because the thought sickens me. I'm dashing forward, tearing through flesh. I hear their screams, but I try not to think about the voices, the lives behind them.

I dodge a fireball directed straight for my heart. I don't know who sent it my way. Maybe Liv. Maybe someone else. I'm focused too intently on simply *surviving*.

My fist makes contact with bone, and I hear it snap. I hear screams and howls, cursing and incantations. Spells spoken in Latin echo in my mind. I don't comprehend what's being said, and I don't give their words another thought. I need to fight my way off Mamá's land and back into the forest. Will and I can reach the manor before the sun rises as long as we move quickly.

I come face to face with an unfamiliar witch. I know she will be an easy kill. The frightened look in her eyes will not haunt me. I will take her life far too easily, and I will succumb to the darkness every vampire must face in order to do it.

In the blink of an eye, I'm before her, but the moment I slash to end her life, claws lengthened and drool dripping down my chin like I'm some rabid beast, something stops me. A blast of fire meant only as a warning assaults my chest. I fall to the ground, instinctively patting my jacket to put out the embers. The fire witch easily could have taken my life, but she didn't. Why?

From where I lie on the ground, I glance up. Liv towers over me. Her gaze is hard, but something softer lingers there. Silently, she begs me to stop fighting. How can she ask me to roll over and die? Where is the dignity in that? And does she really think that's something I could do? It's as if she doesn't know me at all. Maybe she doesn't anymore, because the girl she's become is nothing like the witch I once knew.

If she's not going to play nice, then neither will I. I kick my legs forward, striking her in the ankles. I hit her far harder than intended, and a wave of guilt washes over me as she yelps when she falls to the ground. She breaks her fall with her hands and tumbles over. Her head smacks the frozen ground, and she grunts in response. Dazed, she lies still beside me.

I scramble to my feet, prepared to do whatever necessary to save my soul from eternal damnation. I don't have time to think about how insane it is that I'm fighting my former best friend, especially considering I was ready to sacrifice everything to locate her.

I fought the vampires and was nearly exiled because of my belief that Liv was innocent and didn't deserve to die just because of her association with me. And now we're dueling to the death. Although I will admit, I'm doing that really poorly. If she were any other witch, I would have killed her by now. I wouldn't be twirling around on the ground, hoping this is some wicked nightmare.

"*Suficiente!*" someone yells.

Her words lash out at me the moment her blade pierces my side. Sharp, cold, and brutal, it sinks into my gut like I was soft butter. I feel every inch of metal scraping against flesh. I howl as it enters me, knees buckling. I fall to the ground, blinking away the pain. My kneecaps smack against the earth, and a fierce cramp radiates up my thighs. The icy earth digs into my jeans, soaking the material through.

My heart is pulsating in my mind, and my chest is heaving. My vision is blurry, but I feel the exact moment she places her foot against my back and uses her strength to push my wounded body off her weapon.

I collapse forward. Not bothering to catch myself, I fall against the ground. The grass is dead and dry, the frost coating my mouth and tasting like dirt. I suck in a sharp breath, lungs filling with the fluffy, light snow that is shimmering as flurries fall around me. I choke on it as it melts and hack to relieve myself.

With each cough, the stabbing sensation in my side grows stronger. I wince when it becomes too much to bear. I feel myself healing, my flesh tethering together like braided hair. I was careless. It takes far too much strength to heal myself, and even though there is an endless supply of blood nearby, I worry what I'll become if I taste it.

Someone reaches for me and guides me onto my back. I roll over and arch away from the ground, gasping as the frozen earth brushes against my fresh wound, and I stare into a familiar set of cold, hard irises.

"Abuela," I whisper in disbelief.

My grandmother has been away for the many months I've been a vampire. Having witnessed my coven's initial downfall the night I died, she left the country on her usual trip to visit distant relatives I've never met and have no intention of ever bringing into this dark world I currently inhabit.

Papá always wanted me to leave with her, to learn the old ways of our people, but after he died, Mamá refused. She was too afraid she'd lose me too. Unfortunately, Abuela didn't care for her excuses, and that was Mamá's first mistake. Abuela is a force to be reckoned with, and Mamá's refusal to leave my side after witnessing her husband's demise was considered a disgrace to what he stood for.

When Papá was alive, he and Mamá were set to lead our coven, but after he died, Abuela refused to relinquish control to her. She hoped to one day pass the torch to me, even though I made it clear I had no intention of leading this coven.

Now I stare into her eyes, and I feel my blood run cold. I've always been afraid of my grandmother. She is a fierce woman who is unafraid of vampires. When I was a child, I watched her kill one who was hunting in the woods. This was after Papá died, and watching her slice through the vampire's gut, penetrating his heart, was a bit too graphic for my young eyes. Even so, her strength inspired me to become the hunter I am today. I should thank her. She's one of the reasons I'm still alive.

"Enough of this, *niña*," my grandmother says. "*No más.*"

My throat tightens as she stares down at me, her lip quivering from her anger. Her steely gaze is cold, and it penetrates deep into my soul. I want to fight back, to surprise her with my own strength and power, but I can't. I'm frozen in place by her hatred alone.

Will screams, catching my attention. I search for him in the distance, hoping he is close enough to the forest to escape this mess. Even if I didn't survive, knowing he did would grant my soul peace.

When I see him on the ground, bloody and burned, my mind goes numb. He's crouching on all fours, with swirling streams of magic cascading all around him.

He's flung upward, and he rests his butt on the heels of his feet. His knees rest against the ground, and his face betrays his pain. He's bleeding and bruised, and slowly, his magic attempts to restore him.

The witch magic surrounding him slithers around his feet and hands, threading together, keeping him in place. He struggles to release himself, but every time he does, his enemies approach him, chanting louder, and he cries out. Eventually, he gives up, head lolling to the side, but his gaze never reaches me.

"Will!" I shout.

He does not look at me. Instead, he slumps over, defeated.

"What's happening?" I ask. I glance at the others, but no one will look at me.

When I search the crowd and find my mother, I ask her what's happening.

"*Mamá? Qué estás haciendo?*" I ask, but she does not respond.

"Stand, *niña*," Abuela says.

Although I'm angry and in desperate need of answers, I still obey. A chilling rush washes over me when she speaks. The sensation is eerily familiar to the many times I've participated in past coven rituals. Abuela orders, and I must comply. It's instinctual.

Teetering on my feet, I hold on to my wounded side. The blood curdles in my hand, and I grunt as my torso stretches in my attempt to stand tall.

The witches' chanting grows louder. The stream of magic shoots toward me, assaulting my body with such force, I nearly skid backward on my heels. I dig them into the ground, proving I can withstand the brunt of their fury.

Just like with Will, the witches' magic slithers toward me like a snake on the prowl. It strikes, lashing out and slinking around my limbs. I screech, trying to shake it off. I scratch at my arms, but it's no use. The magic has coated my body, and it will take much more than my feeble swipes to remove it.

When their snaking magic finally ceases its assault, I'm bound by my wrists, just like Will. Thankfully, my feet are free, and I consider my options. Could I outrun them? Even if I could, I would have to abandon Will. Could I live with myself if I knowingly left him to his demise?

Their invisible magic twists tightly around my hands, threading through my fingers and lacing around my palms. It squeezes my arms tightly, painfully together, and I wince as my shoulders tighten, objecting.

"What are you doing? What is this?" I ask, looking at Mamá. She might refuse to speak to me now, but she can't avoid me forever. I will keep reminding her that she's attempting to murder her *daughter*. She can't possibly be such a monster.

"Do not speak unless spoken to, child," Abuela orders.

Ignoring her, I glance at Will, who is still seated on the ground. With hands and feet bound, he looks up at me. My heart breaks for the little boy he's becoming before me. No longer strong, he's scared and hurt. He knows he's on his deathbed, and like me, he's not ready to die.

"I'm so sorry," I whisper to him. Tears prickle behind my eyes, but I do not release them. I won't give the witches power over my emotions any longer.

"Ava," Mamá says, catching my attention.

I jerk my head to look at her. "Mamá..." I whisper, my voice in disbelief. How has it come to this?

"*Vas a estar bien*," she says, but I don't believe her. How will I be okay? How will this be fine?

"*Por favor, Mamá, dime qué está pasando*," I beg. I just need to know what's happening to us. What magic is this? It feels dark and unnatural. My skin itches where it rests against me. And what do the witches plan to do to two hybrids?

"While your grandmother was away, she uncovered the ancient magic of our people," Mamá explains.

"Yes, apparently it is up to me to correct the errors of this coven," Abuela says, glaring at Mamá. My mother cowers under the gaze of her high priestess.

A flash of rage erupts within me. Why is this *her* fault? Why has no one blamed the rogue vampires for this mess? If not for them, no one would be here right now.

"What kind of ancient magic?" I ask. I steal a glance at Will, who seems as utterly confused as I am. The binding on my wrists wraps tighter, and I grind my teeth, groaning. It's a warning, but I won't be silenced.

"A cursed prophecy about a creature—half-dark and half-light," Mamá says. "You cannot remain both, *mija*, and this dark spell will correct that."

"We will reverse this abomination," Abuela says. Her words are laced with anger, and they lash out at me. I too cower beneath her stare, frustrated that she ignites such an instinctual reaction from me.

"We weren't expecting the other," Mamá says, glancing at Will, "but we will return him to his destined path too."

"I don't understand," I say. "What magic? What path?

What are you going to do to us?"

"We will suppress your vampire halves," Abuela says. "It will be as if it no longer exists."

"But... it *does* exist. The vampire is part of me. Mamá, please don't do this."

"*Cállate, niña,*" Mamá says, silencing me. "This must be done."

"If you remove our vampire halves, what's left?" Will asks, finally speaking. He sounds... intrigued, but I must be misreading his emotions. He has to be as frightened as I am right now. The binding on my wrists is making it difficult to think clearly. It digs deeper into my flesh, and soon it will cut through skin.

"*La bruja,*" Abuela says.

I swallow the knot that forms in my throat and glance at Will. He eyes me curiously, not understanding my grandmother.

"The witch," I whisper.

"To complete this spell, I must link the unfortunates to another. Sacrifices, step forward," Abuela orders.

Mamá walks to me, never breaking my gaze when she says, "I will link with my daughter."

"*Y el chico?*" Abuela asks.

No one steps forward to save Will, and for a brief moment, I fear what that will mean. I don't understand this link or its purpose, but I'm certain not having one at all means an untimely death when it comes time to perform the spell.

After several seconds pass, and after I've silently pleaded with just about every witch chaining me to this place, someone steps forward. I'm not surprised by her desire to help, because not even a half hour ago, Will risked his life in an attempt to save hers.

"Liv, are you sure?" Mamá asks. "Do you understand what this means?"

Liv nods but doesn't look at Will or me. Perhaps her shame is getting the best of her. It may be petty, but I hope that feeling haunts her every day for the rest of her life.

"We must hurry," Abuela says. "The sun is rising."

I stare at the sky. In the distance, it grows lighter. I watch as the sun begins to rise, the world erupting in a fury of light as the darkness is cast away. Every second that passes, I see the blanket of sunlight cascading the land, encroaching far too close to my uncovered skin.

Will fights against his restraints as he too watches the sun rise. I still have so many questions for him, not just about what we are and what our magic can do, but also, I want to know about *him*. What is his story? Was his former coven as messed up as mine is? How long has he been searching for another hybrid to spend his days with? Does he regret meeting me? And as the sun begins to rise in the distance, I fear I will never have answers to the many questions circling my mind.

"What if the spell doesn't work?" I cry out, hoping someone, *anyone* will answer me. I don't understand what's happening, but I do know vampires can't survive sunlight. We all know what will happen when that sunlight graces my skin.

"*Entonces morirás,*" Abuela says, utterly emotionless at the thought of losing her only grandchild.

"Mamá!" I scream. "Stop this! Stop it now!"

But it's too late. My mother is ignoring me, choosing to focus instead on murdering her daughter.

The witches have closed in on us, and they link hands now. They're so close. If I weren't frozen in place, held by invisible, magical restraints, I could save myself. But every time I try to break free, the bindings slice into my flesh. Blood drips in steady streams down my hands, splattering onto the icy ground.

A pool of blood sits at Will's feet. He stares into the distance, ignoring the witches completely as he watches the sunrise. I can't see his face, but I'm sure it displays my level of fear. If the witches' magic fails, we will combust, our lives ending in a blazing inferno. That's not exactly the way I want to go.

The crunch of frozen snow under steps distracts me from watching Will, and I jerk my head around to see who's approaching. Mamá is close enough now to touch me, but she does not. Liv is walking closer to Will but at a much more cautionary pace. She doesn't trust him, but she offers her life up as a link. Does she truly feel such guilt?

I look into the forest, hoping to see the familiar set of crimson irises I so desperately need right now, but I know they will not be there. The vampires will not venture out with the sun rising. That's certain death. If Will and I plan to escape, we must do so on our own.

"*Extiende tus brazos, hija,*" Mamá says.

I turn back toward her, confused.

"Hm? What?" I say.

"Hold out your arms," she repeats.

I frown and glance down. My arms are dangling in front of me, blood dripping down my skin, coating my hands and nails. When I glance up at her, her demeanor has changed. She is angry, aggressive.

"Give me your arms, or die from the sun," Mamá orders.

Eyes wide with fear, I nod and hold them up to her. I swallow hard and gnaw on my lower lip. I don't dare look at

Will. Either he will comply, or he will die. Either way, I do not want to watch what is about to happen to us.

The witches chant in Latin, and I struggle to understand them. It's been so long since I've even thought about the Latin language, and I'm too rusty to focus on this foreign spell.

The four of us—Mamá, Liv, Will, and I—are the only beings at the center of the witches' circle. The altar is a few feet away from me, and it is adorned with many things I recognize and some I do not. Relics to represent the elements are placed at the four corners of the altar top, and in the center, a bright, golden sphere represents the sun. In a jar, I see something black, a tarry substance that makes my skin crawl. I've never seen it before, so I don't know its purpose.

Mamá begins to chant as well, but I ignore her too. The blanket of sunlight is close now, and the world is becoming alight. I have only minutes left to live, so with shaky legs and a sputtering heart, I take this time to close my eyes and clear my mind. I try not to cry or beg. I don't want to be weakened in these final moments.

Ignoring the witches' banter, I try to be at peace with my life and with my decisions that led me here. I may have upset the vampires and made mistakes, but I can walk into the flames of death with a clear conscience. The witches never deserved my respect or my loyalty, but helping them in their times of need was the right thing to do. Sometimes we have to cast aside our differences for the greater good, even if that means our own downfall.

Mamá uses my distraction to her benefit, and with my arms held out before me, she finishes her spell, linking our souls by way of the sun's strength. The great ball of fire in the sky is more powerful than even the moon, and I don't need to understand their spell to know they are committing an irreversible act against Will and me.

"My will be done," Mamá says.

A cold chill works its way down my spine as I slowly turn to look at my mother. I remember this moment. It has haunted me since the night I foresaw it. Even so, I am not prepared for the moment a sudden flash of silver radiates across my vision. The blade is brought down, slicing through my flesh, leaving a large crimson gash in its wake.

The moment the blade slashes my forearm, I jolt back to reality. I scream as Mamá digs her fingers into my deeper flesh. When I open my eyes, I watch through blurred vision as she squeezes her free hand into a tight grasp. Droplets of her blood drip into my open body, snaking its way into my veins.

I shriek, engulfed in pain so great it feels as though my soul is being ripped from my body.

I'm falling, yanking myself free from her grasp. I'm on my knees, my lungs burning, tears streaming down my cheeks. My throat is coarse as I howl at the sun, begging for the moon. Chest heaving, I'm not able to catch my breath.

I feel hollow inside, trapped within my own skin. I am sure this is death.

Mamá is crouching beside me. Her lips are moving, so I know she is chanting. But I can't hear her words over the crashing beats of my overworked heart. My head is spinning, my gut churning, and my mind is numbing to the sensations around me.

The world is falling silent. The wind is growing harsh against my skin. My legs feel paralyzed beneath me, and my skin that touches the frozen ground is numbing. The pain in my arm dulls, but the agony of what remains spreads through my body like a rapid brush fire. It seeps into every crevice of my body. From toe to crown and from fingertips to my very core, I am losing my sensations and my will to survive.

Slowly, I begin to connect and awaken again, but the world is different. It feels . . . boring, bland, and lifeless. I don't hear the creatures, I don't smell the forest, but I do feel the cold. It aches from my skin deep into my bones. It settles within me, and I begin to shake. Lip quivering, I see my breath as bursts of lacy steam puffs.

"With the success of this spell, the abominations will have no access to their dark abilities. They become one with their links from now until the end," Abuela says.

My grandmother's words loop in my mind, but only when Mamá steps away and the witches break their binds do I fully understand their meaning.

The witches smile and celebrate all around me, but I cannot focus. I'm too distracted by the empty, hollow pit of despair that encompasses my entire essence. Inside, I remain in shadows. The darkness that was once my vampire half is still there, but it is severed from me. Forever out of reach but so close, I experience the pain of loss over and over again. The vampire within me steadily breaks away, and I mourn her again and again.

I do nothing to save her. I don't reach out and grab on to her hand. I don't try to pull her back to me. I don't scream for her return or try to mold her with the witch, with the *thing* that remains inside me.

Even though I want to, I don't do these things because I'm staring at the sky, shielding my eyes from the sun, which cascades over my entire body, brightening my pale, luminescent skin.

I blink and it's still there, shining down on me.

This is not a dream or a nightmare or a vision.

This is real life.

The spell awakened the witch by smothering the vampire, and now, I live once again.

In sunlight.

ALSO BY DANIELLE ROSE

DARKHAVEN SAGA

Dark Secret

Dark Magic

Dark Promise

Dark Spell

Dark Curse

PIECES OF ME DUET

Lies We Keep

Truth We Bear

**For a full list of Danielle's other titles,
visit her at DRoseAuthor.com**

ACKNOWLEDGMENTS

I'm eternally grateful that I am able to make writing a full-time career, and I know that wouldn't be possible without the incredible support system I have. I love each and every one of you.

To Shawna — I think we met by fate and not a day goes by that I'm not grateful for your friendship. You're the person I vent to when things get tough, and you're never afraid to tell me when I'm being ridiculous. I appreciate your honesty and candor, and I love you and all your crazy crochet-slash-anime obsessions. Also, I miss your face.

To Heather and Robin — You're the reason I even have a career. Those who work silently in the background are the most unappreciated and often go unnoticed, but not you two. I shout from the rooftops how much I adore you both. Thanks for always being there for me.

To my family — you show me unquestionable support, even when I say things like, "I want to quit my job and try writing full-time!" Publishing is a tough industry. At times, it's soul-crushing, and I wouldn't be able to wipe away the tears without you. I love you.

To my readers — I *literally* couldn't do this job without you. A writer is nothing without a reader, and I never forget that. From the bottom of my heart, *thank you*.

To my Waterhouse Press family — I am so proud to be

part of this family. I can't wait for everything that's to come. Thank you for trusting me and welcoming me with open arms.

Special thanks to my editor, Scott, who is quite possibly the most patient man on this planet. 2019 wasn't an easy year for me, but you were always there to offer support and encouragement. *Thank you.*

ABOUT DANIELLE ROSE

Dubbed a "triple threat" by readers, Danielle Rose dabbles in many genres, including urban fantasy, suspense, and romance. The *USA Today* bestselling author holds a master of fine arts in creative writing from the University of Southern Maine.

Danielle is a self-professed sufferer of 'philes and an Oxford comma enthusiast. She prefers solitude to crowds, animals to people, four seasons to hellfire, nature to cities, and traveling as often as she breathes.

Visit her at DRoseAuthor.com

CONTINUE READING
THE DARKHAVEN SAGA

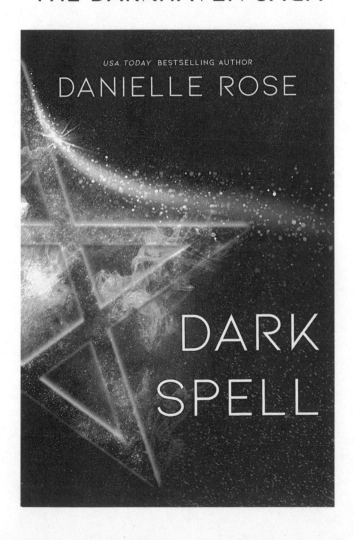